HAUNTED LIGHTHOUSES

AND 20 MORE HORROR SHORT STORIES

GREG STRANDBERG

Big Sky Words Press, Missoula

First paperback printing, 2022

Printed in the United States of America

ISBN: 9798842050253

ALSO BY GREG STRANDBERG

The Jongurian Mission

Trouble in Jonguria

The Jongurian Resolution

The Warring States

The State of Chu

The State of Qin

Tarot Card Killer

Black Walnut

Room 223

The Hirelings

Wake Up, Detroit

Ale Quest

Nine Amusing Tales

G.I. JOE: The Dreadnoks

G.I. JOE: JOE Team-13

G.I. JOE: After Infinity

G.I. JOE: To Its Knees

Florida Sinkholes

Bring Back Our Girls

Lightning

Fire

Dulce Base

CONTENTS

1. THE SEGUIN ISLAND LIGHTHOUSE

Seguin Island is a rocky and desolate affair, and enough to drive a sane person mad. To say you could use something to lighten up the mood is an understatement. And while stories and drink have long been used to pass the time, so too has song.

That's what Edgar James thought when he and his wife Ella were serving as lighthouse keepers there in the 1850s. After several months of the melancholy atmosphere it was clear to James that he had to find something to lighten the mood.

James managed to scrape together what meager savings he had, and on a rare trip to the mainland and the city of Portland twenty-three miles to the northwest he bought Ella a square grand piano.

He took great care in transporting it and having it installed in the small cottage affixed to Seguin Island Lighthouse. This required James to take Ella out on a long stroll around the island, something she found rather odd since James was always complaining how much he'd come to despise the place.

She finally convinced him to head back, and after what he judged a fair amount of time he relented. His wife headed into the cottage, a little angry that she was starting supper so late, when she saw the large square grand sitting there in the open space before the hearth.

"Oh James!" she cried, falling into his arms and the rushing up to the instrument.

James knew she hadn't had lessons in some time, but she quickly took to the one piece of sheet music that the store owner had thrown in, "Miss Lucy Long," sometimes called "Take Your Time Miss Lucy."

The lighthouse took on a merry glow as Ella played into the night, and James was content now that happiness had come again.

It didn't last long, however. Ella played the tune first thing the next morning, waking James up. He smiled and rose and got about the day, but returned at lunch to hear it again, and then at supper too.

Each day was the same, with Ella playing "Miss Lucy" nonstop. He asked her to try another tune, something she may still remember from her youth, but either she couldn't or wouldn't. It began to grate on James, and the desolate landscape wasn't the only thing grating at his soul.

A month went by and "Miss Lucy" continued to 'take her time.' It was a Thursday when James snapped, one that dawned cold and foggy. The mists off Casco Bay were shrouding the land two miles in the distance, and any ships would have a hard time of it indeed trying to get to port near the Kennebec River.

None of that was on James' mind as he headed to the small shed outbuilding, the merry jaunt of "Miss Lucy" coming from the house behind him.

His face was unshaven, his teeth turning yellow. He looked on in a daze, a shambling thing more than a man. Reaching the shed he fumbled at the open lock, finally undoing it before letting it fall to the ground. Inside he found what he was looking for and grasped it tightly.

The music rose to its climax as he neared the house. The pause came, the fanfare, and ending. James stopped, something inside of him resting finally. It lasted a brief moment before the song started anew. Something inside of him died at the sound, and he clutched the prize in his hand tighter.

Inside Ella pounded away at the keys, the mesmerizing melody producing an eerie euphoria in her that ate away at the desolateness that had plagued her soul for so long. She didn't even hear the screen door crash or the footsteps of her husband behind her. She hadn't in some time.

Her playing increased, a frantic pitch like a demon's wail, and from behind her James clutched the double-headed axe in his hands. The head gleamed in the soft glow of the single candle's light.

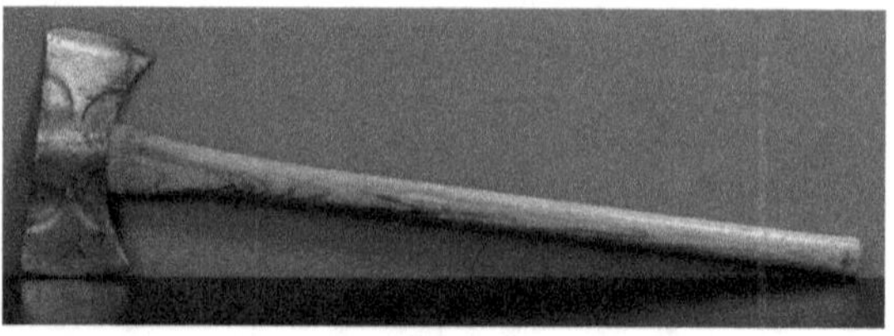

His mouth made to move, trying to will the words from his mind into life, the words he'd been unable to say no matter how much he'd wanted to. *Stop! For the love of God, woman, STOP!*

Ahead of him Ella played on, as if she knew what her husband was trying to say and agreed with him, but the only way she could acknowledge such, and indeed agree with it, was to play on all the harder, all the faster, and all out like her life depended on it. In a way it did.

The last vestiges of hope escaped James and he raised the axe up, then moved forward. With a single mighty heave he brought the axe down on Ella's hands, just as they'd reached the triple-key affair that he'd first loved so much upon first listen.

Ella screamed as her fingers were severed from her hands and blood sprayed over the white keys, black too. But it wasn't a scream of pain, more a scream in line with the music, as if she was trying to replace the sounds lost from her hands with that still available from her voice.

It wasn't the reaction James had wanted, if indeed he'd wanted anything. He was guided by something else now. Outside the waves crashed upon the rocky shore.

James pulled the axe back and swung it at Ella, severing her head with one clean swipe. Her hands still motioned as if playing, even as her body teetered back and fell to the floor. The song, however, would not end, at least not in whatever mind James was hearing from.

He brought the axe down on the square grand piano, first on the large wooden top, splintering it but not breaking it. He swung again and again and wood and chips and splinters began to fly. On the floor his wife bled everywhere from the neck. Her head was nowhere in sight.

It took nearly three minutes for James to chop the piano to bits, at least enough for his liking. He was filled with a primal desire and also a sense of fulfillment. He was in ecstasy.

He looked down at the axe, all covered in saw dust, but still showing splotches of red as well. He brought it up slowly to his chest, touched it a few times to where his heart was, then brought it back down. A wicked grin came to his face, then faded quickly as his frame lurched and his muscles worked.

He brought the axe up as fast as he could and the razor-sharp head embedded itself into his heart. He fell to the floor dead next to his wife's decapitated body and the piano they'd both 'loved' so much.

THE END

2. HAUNTED LIGHTHOUSES

There's something about the sea and the lighthouses that watch her that bring out the ghosts.

Maybe it's the sudden and unexpected ways that so many have died near lighthouses in the past. Perhaps it's anger over the light not protecting them as it should, or even anger over a spot where a light should have been long ago when the coasts in whatever particular area were still barren of man's imprint.

It seems a psychic imprint of energy is left behind when these deaths at sea and near shore occur. Residue is leftover, typically not for the better. Sometimes it's just a spirit that can't find its way to the other side. Other times, however, there's a more diabolical intent.

And so it is that we have tales of hauntings in lighthouses the world over.

The Great Lakes of North America are a prime spot for haunted lighthouses. Michigan's Upper Peninsula is a good place to visit. Big Bay Point Lighthouse was built there to protect that area and the ships moving past its rugged coastline. She was completed in 1896 and William Prior was assigned the role of the light's first keeper.

Things went well for William. His teenage son, George, served as his assistant. But then tragedy came a year after they took the job. George was atop the light one day when he stumbled and fell down the stairs. His leg got slashed open, exposing the bone. They got him to the hospital, but it was too late – George died that night.

William was devastated. He went back to the light, but all the old cheer was gone. He became depressed and despondent and no longer cared about life. It wasn't long before he disappeared, leaving the light vacant. No one knew where he went…until a year and a half later.

That's when they found his skeleton hanging from a tree in the forest behind the light. He'd killed himself…or more aptly, the grief had.

Ever since then, visitors to Big Bay Point Lighthouse have reported strange happenings. Cabinets often slam on their own. Sometimes a ghost can be seen walking the lighthouse grounds. It's always wearing a U.S. Life Saving service uniform. Just like William Prior always wore.

Many hauntings can be traced back to some long ago tragedy. That's the case with South Manitou Island Lighthouse that guards the Straits of Mackinac.

It's a remote island, barren, with little life and nothing to sustain humans. So the keepers of the light were forced to make frequent trips by boat to the mainland for supplies. In rough seas, this could be treacherous. That was the case on one terrible day in 1878.

The lighthouse's first keeper was named Aaron Sheridan. He and his wife Julia were staying at the light, along with their infant son. They had to make a supply run, the seas were too rough, their boat capsized, and all three drowned. Ever since then there have been unexplained noises at the light. Some hear echoing voices, others the sounds of footsteps.

Many ghost aficionados say that Point Lookout Lighthouse in Maryland is the most haunted lighthouse there is. She was built in 1830 on the western shores of the Chesapeake Bay, right at the entrance to the Potomac River. Her first thirty years were largely uneventful. Then the Civil War came. A military hospital and a prison camp were located near the light. Both were overcrowded and suffered from disease. Those that didn't die in the fighting often suffered an even worse fate in the prison camp. Those that went to the hospital usually experienced excruciatingly painful amputations, typically without pain-killing drugs. The operations killed many.

Is it any surprise there's a bit of paranormal activity in the area? This has filtered to the nearby Point Lookout Lighthouse. Ghosts of all types and ages have been seen at the light, mainly at the top of the building or in the basement. Doors and windows will open and close on their own. Visitors hear voices and footsteps, even snoring.

There are many more lighthouses around the world with similar stories. This book tells many of their stories.

3. CALLING BLOODY MARY

"And don't you even *think* about moving from that spot until I come get you in the morning!"

Amber flinched away from Gary's raised fist, huddled deeper into her blankets, stuffed animals, and whatever else was on the floor. The chain that secured her foot to the floor rattled slightly as she moved.

"I don't want to hear that damn chain again tonight!" Gary said before heading out of the laundry room. He slammed the door to drive his point home.

Amber kept her head buried in the blankets for a few moments more, then looked up at the door…waited…

CLICK!

The door was locked from the other side. Gary was taking longer to do that these days, though he wasn't leaving it open anymore…not since that night.

Amber shrugged off her blankets and then looked down at her legs. The bruising wasn't that bad this time. But then after seven years, she was getting used to it.

"Oh…God…" she moaned as the realization of what that thought actually meant dawned on her. Not for the first time, she cried herself to sleep.

~~~

Amber awoke with a start and shot up from her makeshift bed on the floor. Her eyes went to the small window near the ceiling, and she
~~~

saw it was still dark. She had no idea what time it was since Gary didn't allow a clock in the small room, but if she had to guess she'd say it was well into morning, probably 3 AM or so.

"It's time," she said to herself out loud, as if to steel her resolve. She'd been meaning to go through with this ever since that night a few weeks back when Gary had let her watch TV for a bit. It'd been the first time in nearly a year, and what she'd seen had amazed her.

Could it be real? The thought bounced around in her head as she reached over for her favorite stuffed animal, a one-eyed yellow bunny left over from three Easter's ago. His name was "Mr. Cooper" and Amber carefully began to work her fingers over his left foot, feeling for...*there!*

She began to work the straightened paperclip out of Mr. Cooper's foot and soon had the one-and-a-half-inch wire in front of her. Amber began to work on the lock securing her to the floor, careful to put a blanket under the chain and the bare wood. She didn't want to wake Gary...not again.

It took several minutes of delicate work, and then finally there was the 'snap.' The lock came open. Amber's eyes went wide, just as they had the first time she'd tried, on the trial run. Tonight it was for real, she kept reminding herself, and that meant she only had this one chance.

What if it doesn't work? She quickly shook the thought from her head. If it didn't work she was in for a heck of a beating, nothing more. Gary wouldn't kill her – he'd learned that lesson real good with Sheryl.

Amber slowly undid the chain from her leg, then rose up and started toward the door. It was locked, but what Gary didn't know is that she had a key. Reaching over to the doorframe, she ran her fingers over the wallpaper until coming to a slight tear. There was a separation there, and carefully working her two fingers in, she pulled out the credit card she'd stolen from Gary's wallet that time it'd fallen out overnight. Oh how she'd taken a beating when he'd not found that card, but he never could pin the theft of it on her.

"Never leave home without it," Amber said with a sly smile, remembering one of the TV advertisements she'd heard as a young girl at her parent's home. Ages ago now.

She slipped the credit card into the door and began working at the lock. She knew that it wouldn't–

CLICK!

For the second time that night, Amber's eyes went wide with surprise. This was really working!

Her heart racing, Amber slowly pulled open the door…looked out into the hallway. She hadn't been out in weeks, not even to the bathroom – Gary kept a baby potty in the room for her. She was going to the bathroom now, however, for that was the closest room in the house with what she sought…a mirror.

She'd remembered hearing something about the story when she was younger, in her other life when she'd still been at school. Seeing the show on the TV, however, that'd opened her eyes to the possibilities. *And so what if she takes me,* Amber thought to herself as she slowly made her way down the hallway, toward the dark bathroom that lay at the end, *death can't possibly be any worse than this.*

Amber made it to the bathroom and moved her hand up to the light at the wall…then stopped herself. *No,* she thought, *it* has *to be black…it* has *to be right.*

She went inside and closed the door. She moved to the counter, put her hands up next to where the sink was. It was pitch black, she couldn't see anything, but she knew…she knew that a huge wall mirror was before her. There was no medicine cabinet behind it, just a hunk of reflective glass that had been secured there by Gary or whoever had originally built this house. Amber stared into it, and then started to speak.

"Bloody Mary…Bloody Mary…Bloody Mary."

She still had the paperclip from the room and, with a wince, stuck her thumb with its small end. It hurt, but it drew blood. She reached her bloody thumb out and touched the mirror, then moved it around and touched four more times, making a square.

Amber could feel something…some kind of…*presence.* She reached her hand down and turned on the tap. The sound of running water filled the bathroom.

"This is the cleanser of the dead," she said aloud, putting her hands over her eyes, "I wish to speak with the fallen queen."

"Queen of falling blood…Queen of hatred…"

Amber's heart raced at the words she heard, deathly words, hollow and full of dread. She felt herself getting scared, but resolved herself. *Death can't possibly be any worse than this.*

Amber removed her hands from her eyes. The bathroom was

pitch black, but she knew…she knew she wasn't alone.

"Bloody Mary," Amber began, in a firm voice that she hoped didn't betray her fear, "I need your–"

BANG!

The bathroom door slammed open and light shot into the room. Amber turned to look, her eyes wide, and in the split second before the door hit her she saw Gary standing there, the light of the hallway illuminating him. She saw more, though…she saw *her*.

~~~

"Get out of the way, get out of the way!"

The medics yelled and jostled and people got the message. The route cleared and there was soon a path to the awaiting ambulance. Within moments they had the young girl inside, and then the siren was wailing and they were racing to the hospital.

"Think she'll be alright?"

The head medic looked to his assistant and nodded. "She will be, physically at least. Mentally…I don't know."

"What could have caused that back there…we know she had to have fallen and knocked herself out on the bathtub. There's no way she could have done that to him."

"I know," the head medic said as he looked down at the young girl before him, still unconscious. The strength required to rip a man apart like that…she *couldn't* have done it.

Then what did?

The medic tried not to think about it, tried to only listen to the sirens coming from above.

THE END
~~~

4. SMOKING PORCH

I've been smoking for years, so it was a real pain when the new place I moved into didn't allow it inside. Instead, they had a smoking porch out back. The landlord had chuckled when he'd shown it to me. "Lots of people end up quitting after moving in here," he'd said.

I thought nothing of it…at the time. Despite my love of nicotine and the comfort of smoking indoors, the place was ideal…and I was ready for a move. I just couldn't take California and their restrictions anymore, and with the freedom my job gave me, I chose the backwoods, flyover part of the country.

The apartment I was renting was in an old house that'd been converted into five units – two upstairs, two down, and one in the basement. In the back was a porch, though not connected to any of the units. To reach it, you had to walk out back and then up the rickety set of steps. It gave a good view of the small creek that ran through the even smaller backyard. Beyond that it was forested hills as far as the eye could see.

I spent a lot of time on the porch. I was a remote worker now, had been since the pandemic. I didn't need to be in the office, was no longer held to the 15-minute-break-every-two-hours routine that most in the rat race had to put up with. Now I could smoke every fifteen minutes, like I preferred.

So I did, out back on the porch…come rain or shine, sun or snow. It was peaceful out there by day, nothing but the babbling of the small stream, some birds chirping, maybe the occasional car passing by out front on the street that didn't see a lot of traffic.

Night, however, was a different story. It was dark out back, pretty much pitch black if there was no moon. The only light was one of those flesh detector's that went on if a person walked into view. The landlord was kinda cheap too, so it had a short timer. That meant when I was done smoking and walking back, it'd typically go off just seconds after I was out of view.

It always gave me an eerie sensation.

One night in early-summer I headed out to do my thing. It was balmy, not too-hot and just right for wearing shorts. Crickets chirped somewhere nearby, accompanied by the buzzing of other nighttime insects. The light flicked-on as I approached, illuminating the typical scene of grass, stream, and trees. I settled into one of the comfy chairs, lit up, and let my thoughts go.

Then the light went off.

My eyes went wide at the sudden blanket of darkness that fell upon me. *That* had never happened before. My first thought was that the light had just burned out. But then, as if reading my thoughts, it flashed back on…but only for a second. Still, it was long enough for me to catch sight of…*it.*

I really don't know how to describe it.

It wasn't a man and it wasn't an animal. It was humanoid, with legs that seemed to come *from* the earth, or were at least attached *to* it. So were the ends of its arms. I couldn't rightly call *them* hands. And it's head. It was almost like some kind of ooze was coming off it. The whole *creature* was dark and shadowed, even in the bright light of that one second, like even that force shied away from it.

I froze after that second, the cigarette halfway up to my mouth. My eyes began to water in fear, though I couldn't take them from the spot where the *thing* had been.

Then the light flashed on again, just for a split-second this time, like a strobe. My eyes widened even further. The *thing* was stopped now, and its head had turned and it was looking *directly at me!*

My heart raced and my blood seemed to freeze. I could feel the tears of fear coursing down my cheeks. All motor function was gone. My body was stiff and I couldn't have moved if I'd wanted to. And my God, did I want to! Every fiber of my being told me to bolt-up and run away, run as fast as I could away from that…that…*thing.* But I couldn't. I couldn't move a muscle, couldn't lift a finger.

As if to mock me, and perhaps reading my thoughts, the light flashed again, an even quicker strobe this time, just a quarter of a second.

This time the thing was closer to me, to the steps of the porch. It's hideous body was somehow part of the earth, undulating and moving toward me as some kind of ooze dripped from it. But that's not what sent jolts of fear coursing through me. No, the thing was *smiling* at me. Smiling with what seemed like a million jagged teeth.

I knew I was going to die, I just knew it. Whatever that thing was, it was going to come up those steps and onto the porch and it was going to eat me. There was nothing I could do about this, for I was frozen. Any second now the light would flash on again, this time revealing the creature just inches from my face, that hideous mouth open wide and those jaggedly-sharp teeth dripping their ooze onto me as they dove in for the kill. Any second and–

"Aaaahhhh!!!"

I screamed from the pain of the red hot 1,600 °F cigarette ember burning into the sides of my index and middle fingers. I'd completely forgotten I was holding it, but it'd been burning all the time.

With the scream I jerked, my hands involuntarily doing what my body wouldn't do on its own. I jolted upright, flicked my hand back and forth, and then grasped onto it with my other. In that moment, I completely forgot about the creature.

Then the light flashed on…and stayed on. Before me was the grass and the stream and the trees and hills beyond. There was no creature, not even a trace. But I knew I hadn't imagined it. It was too vivid, too…*real.*

I dashed up from the chair and ran from the smoking porch. I moved out of the apartment the next day. I haven't had a cigarette since.

THE END

5. THE HAUNTINGS OF HECETA HEAD

In some places of the world, the barrier between the living and the dead is thin. In some places it doesn't exist at all. This small pocket of Oregon is one of those places.

May 15, 2022
Heceta Head Lighthouse
Between Yachats and Florence, Oregon

"Alright, alright…gather 'round!"

The Suislaw High School students took a few minutes, but eventually they were all gathered in front of the tour guide. Quite a few snickers and grins accompanied their efforts, though most saved their sighs, knowing this was the last 'lecture' on the lighthouse tour.

"Now," the tour guide said when things had finally quieted down,

"I suppose you want to hear about the ghost."

Things really got quiet then, and every one of the high schoolers' eyes was on the guide. For his part, the guide smiled – there wasn't too much exciting about giving volunteer tours of a lighthouse that'd been built in 1894, but this part was. He waited for a few more moments, letting the tension build, hoping to hell it wouldn't be interrupted by one of those damn cell phones.

"*Ghost?*" one of the students said, mocked was more like it. His tone earned a few chuckles from the students nearby, other jocks by the look of it.

"Ghost*s* might be more apt," the guide said with a smile as he turned around to look up at the top of the lighthouse and the many panes of glass it held, "and we even know one of their names."

"'Know one of their names,'" the student laughed, "how can we know that?"

The guide smiled.

April 12, 1984

BREEP! BREEP! BREEP!

"Goddamn it!" Chester shouted. A moment later Floyd came running into the room.

"I just checked it, boss, I *just* checked it!"

Chester shook his head and rolled his eyes, although carefully. The first time the damn smoke alarm had gone off he'd almost fallen from his ladder. His good pants were already spackled with paint, and he didn't want any more 'mishaps' on this job.

"Well, check it again, will ya!" Chester yelled out so as to be heard over the constant blaring. "In fact," he yelled as Floyd started back down the hallway, "just take the damn batteries out!"

"Got it, boss!" Floyd called back. A minute later the blaring stopped, and Chester shook his head again before getting back to work. They'd been in the lighthouse for just a day now, but not an hour passed that something didn't happen to slow them down. Chester just wanted to get done with it and get back to Newport where the jobs were…more normal. If he had to–

BREEP! BREEP! BREEP!

"Goddamn it!" Chester shouted out again, and it seemed faster than a moment that Floyd came running back in.

"Boss, I *just* took the batteries out of the smoke detector, honest!"

Chester frowned and shook his head. "It's alright, Floyd," he said in a soft voice, one that could barely be heard over the blaring, "let's just get this job done and leave this place alone."

He'd heard the stories of the college kids a decade before. He didn't want to experience what they had.

December 8, 1977

"Ssshhh!"

"Oh, give me a break, Bobby," Diane laughed, "there's *no one* around!"

Even the darkness of the night couldn't hide how embarrassed Bobby's face suddenly became. He shuffled his feet and frowned. "I know, it's just that…"

"You don't like breaking into a lighthouse, I get it," Ron said, that smile of his setting those dimples off. Diane seemed to cozy up to him further, and Bobby shuffled his feet a bit more.

"Just hurry up, will ya? I don't want to be out here!"

"Oh, don't tell me that you're afraid of the dark?" Ron said with a laugh as he wiggled the lockpicking tools a bit more. "Or is it just that you're–"

CLICK!

Ron's words were cutoff as the lock clicked open, and he stared back at his two friends from OSU and smiled. "See, I *told* you it was nothing!"

"Yeah, *forty minutes ago*," Diane said as she rolled her eyes and pushed past her on-again, off-again boyfriend. Within moments she had the door open and was standing in the lighthouse's entryway.

"Guys…are you sure we should be doing this?" Bobby called out to them from where he was still standing outside.

"Feel free to wait outside," Ron called back, and then he and Diane disappeared further inside. Bobby sighed, but followed them in.

They made their way through the lighthouse entryway and to the stairs. They wanted to get up as high as they could, and from what they'd heard, that was the small landing just below the light. That door would be locked to them, and with a lock that couldn't be picked. No matter, their Ouija Board would likely work anywhere.

"Let's get it out and get it done with," Diane said once they'd reached the spot.

"What, is the place starting to trip you out?" Ron laughed.

"Yeah," Diane said with a cold look. Ron frowned and swallowed and got out the board.

"How do we start?" Bobby asked, his curiosity overcoming his fear.

"We have to ask a question," Diane said as she took hold of the planchette, "then we just–"

The planchette jerked Diane's hands forward, first to the letter 'R' then 'U' then 'E.'

Ron stared down at the board, his eyes wide. "Rue?"

That's my name, an ethereal voice said, one that was all around them…everywhere.

The next sound was the three students' feet pounding down the lighthouse stairs. The door to the lighthouse banged back and forth in the wind as they ran for their lives.

August 21, 1977

"Aw hell, Tim…I left my tool belt up in the attic."

Tim shook his head and stared at Dan. "Well, get on up there then, we don't got all day and that traffic on 101 ain't gonna get any better. Go on."

Dan nodded and took off at a run. They were just finishing up for the day and still had two left, but Dan wasn't one to leave his tools behind. He was soon at the largest of the lighthouse grounds' three houses, through the door, and bounding up the stairs. There were two floors and then the attic, where he'd been working that afternoon, sealing up the roof so it'd make it through another harsh, Oregon Coast winter. He was wondering why he'd left his tools when he reached the attic ladder and headed up. They should be right in the corner, near the—"

Dan froze. There before him was what he could only describe as a 'gray lady,' her back to him. She looked like she was from a black and white movie, literally taken off the screen. She had silver hair and a long, dark dress. Her tone and hue were all wrong, and it suddenly dawned on Dan that he was seeing a ghost. He narrowed his eyes and saw that she was staring down at his tools. Just then she began to turn, and Dan was frozen with terror. She faced him, and Dan saw that she had the face of a woman…sort of. She was old, yet young, yet haggard…and *dead*. Just then she smiled, and a chill went through him. Somehow he found his legs and was rushing down the ladder and then out of the house.

February 11, 1933

The winds howled and the gale showed no signs of blowing itself out. Edna looked up at Mike.

"You've got to go out there, you've got to go—"

"I ain't goin' out to that shed again, woman, I ain't goin' nowhere but off this rock as soon as this storm ends."

"You're just seein' things!" Edna said.

"That's right I'm seeing things, and I don't mean to see 'em no more."

Edna gave her husband a hard look. "Those ships *need* that light."

"They'll not be getting it tonight, not from me at least," Mike said. "And what's stoppin' you from goin' out there to the shed and getting it?"

Edna frowned. "Only a fool would go out there after what you saw."

Mike nodded. Finally after all these years, his wife was getting some sense.

April 28, 1892

"This is the spot the Warren's told us of," Roy said as he pulled up on the ox train and brought it to a stop.

"Mighty fine spot for a light," Harp said from further back.

"Aye, that it is, that it is," Roy said. Both he and Harp headed further along the grassy hilltop and put their hands to their foreheads. The sun was shining. They couldn't have asked for a better day to start clearing. Not that there was a lot to clear. A few trees were all the grassy stretch held, and it wouldn't...

"Hey," Roy said, pointing back behind them and near a tree, "what's that?"

"Looks like a rock of some sort," Harp said.

"I ain't never seen no rock standing up like that," Roy said as he started forward, "that's...that's a grave marker."

"Can't be," Harp said as he came up, "the Warren's would have told us about one of their kids dying."

"Maybe it wasn't one of theirs...maybe they don't know about it."

"Injuns don't bury their kids here, you know that."

Roy gave Harp a hard look. "I know that, you fool. Now just come on down here with me and—"

The wind kicked up suddenly, just as Roy was bending down to grab hold of the rock. He looked up, and his eyes went wide. The sky was suddenly dark, and out to sea the waves were higher than he'd ever seen before.

"Uh…I wouldn't do that," Harp said, backing off a bit. In the distance the oxen were growing skittish.

"Alright…let's…let's just call it a day, huh?" Roy said.

"Aye," Harp agreed, and both men were quickly on the beaten path heading back to the woods.

June 4, 1888

"This is the spot," Welcome said, and from across the grassy stretch on top of the hilltop, his wife nodded.

"I'll say it is," Dolly replied with a smile, "home at last, eh?"

Welcome smiled at his wife in return. The Warren's had been granted the 164-acre stretch along the Oregon Coast, and they meant to make good on the claim. It was rocky ground, but inland and along Cape Creek the land was fine for farming.

"Now we just need to get to raising a family to help with all this," Dolly said.

Welcome smiled to that, and went over to take his wife's hand. The wind picked up as they started back toward the woods away from the point. Neither heard the delighted laughter that had followed their pronouncement.

June 29, 1851

Conner stared at his boss, and finally asked the question he'd been meaning to all day.

"What do you want to do, boss?"

James stared at his surveying partner across the fire and shook his head. "Leave it blank."

Conner stared up at him. *"Blank?"*

"Aye," James said, turning back to look out at the Pacific Ocean, and the point protruding not far from their camp, "leave it blank. As far as the federal government is concerned this part of the Siuslaw River doesn't exist, you got that?"

"Boss…how can I just leave out the mouth of the river?"

"Then leave the whole damn thing out, you got that?" James said, giving his subordinate a sharp look. He knew what'd he'd seen that morning when he'd ventured onto that grassy hilltop, damn it. After seeing it he'd known he'd do his part to keep God-fearing men out of here for as long as possible, the ships passing by be damned!

Conner looked up at his boss. They'd surveyed this whole stretch, had done so for months. But then he'd never seen that look in his boss's eye, either. With a nod he put away his pencils and started to roll up his maps. The Siuslaw would remain hidden.

July 16, 1798

Wani jumped up and over the rocks and came to yet another small cove. The waves broke up and high and overhead he could see a small, flat area. He smiled as he looked at the cliffs leading up to it – yet another challenge. All he had to do was start up the small path and then–

"Wapi, no."

Wapi turned around to see his grandmother there. He frowned and cursed his luck – she was supposed to be back on the beach, watching the little ones playing with shells. She nodded up at the small flat area at the top of the cliffs that he'd been looking at, and shook her head.

"You're never to go up there, is that understood?"

Wapi turned his head back and looked again. "Why?"

"There's death up there," his grandmother replied, and it seemed to Wapi as if all the color had gone from her face. "It wasn't always like that, even when they came so long ago." She trailed off for a moment, then shook her head and started to turn. "It's up there now though, whatever it is."

Wapi watched her go, then turned back to look up at the cliffs. He swallowed the knot in his throat that was suddenly there, as well as his earlier plans at exploration. His grandmother knew of the spirit world, and that was enough for him. He turned back, toward the sounds of young Suislaw Indian children laughing on the shore.

May 15, 1775

Don Bruno Heceta stared at the desolate landscape, then lowered his looking glass and turned back to his crew.

"This is the spot," he said, "this is where she will rest."

The crew of the *Santiago* gave some halfhearted nods, and even the first mates looked more resigned to the task than eager to fulfill it. The coast they were on was some of the rockiest they'd seen since leaving Mexico to sail north, and the thought of landing anywhere on it didn't appeal to them. Still, it only took one pass by the captain's cabin, one listen to the crying that was coming from the silver-haired woman within, to know that they had to have some peace.

It took them several hours to find a safe spot to drop anchor, even with the shallower waters the captain had spotted earlier that day. They put the boat over the side, into the choppy and cold water. Not a soul was in sight, on sea or land.

Heceta manned the boat, his most trusted men with him. He had no concern that his remaining crew might abandon him, seize the ship and sail back to Portugal. After the death of his young daughter Rue, born just weeks after leaving the warm, southern climes, he cared about little. It'd hit his wife harder, and he knew that putting the small child to rest would be the best thing for them…he hoped.

The crew powered through the surf and over the final waves. They reached the rocky and shell-strewn beach and Heceta looked up at the towering point above, his dead child cradled in his arms. Without a word he started walking toward the cliffs, hoping to find a path that led up. He was lucky, and a path existed, most likely etched their by whatever Indians called this area home. Heceta hoped he didn't meet any, but didn't really care either.

It took them the better part of an hour to go up the worn path, which really wasn't much of a path at all they realized after going up close to the top. They struggled up the last few feet but made it, and stood on a grassy bluff overlooking the rocky shore.

"It's a beautiful spot, sir," one of the crewman said, and Heceta nodded. That is was.

The men set to work, digging. It didn't take long, for they didn't have to go too deep or too long. Then they were done, and the captain lowered the body of his baby girl into the hole. The men covered the child over, then secured a good-sized rock they'd found on the way up, one flat and long and as close to a gravestone as they were likely to get.

After saying a few words, the men prayed that God would take the child and that she could rest in peace. On the way down the cliffs, Heceta prayed this his wife could find that peace as well. Deep in his soul, however, he knew that in this life she never would.

THE END

6. THE PHONE THAT WASN'T THERE

"The phone that wasn't there," that's what the staff called it.

They'd been calling it that at the Cecil Hotel ever since 1932, when the ringing began.

It was on the fourth floor, though no one was sure if it was Room 408 or 410. It could very well have been Room 409 or 411 across the hall as well, and some were even convinced it was the floor above or even below.

What no one disputed was the sound. It was the typical candlestick telephone ringer sound, a high-pitched bell that clanged in the ringer box.

The phones that'd originally been installed when the Cecil was built in 1924 had been replaced in 1932 with the newer model 202 telephones. Western Electric made them, or at least did until 1937.

They were still widely used until the 1950s, though the Cecil had replaced its 202s with the model 500.

The experts all agreed that it wasn't the 500 that was making the noise, however, but the 202. Yes, the Cecil had called in experts, had done so at least once a decade since the sounds began.

When did the sounds begin?

The first recorded mention of the "phantom ringing," as it was often called in the early days, was on October 2, 1932. One Regina Maxwell, a maid in the hotel, had been cleaning Room 408.

She heard the phone ring and went to pick it up. When she said 'hello,' however, there was no answer. Even more strange, the ringing continued. Ms. Maxwell put the phone down and went to the hallway.

She was sure it'd been the phone in Room 408 but after she'd picked up that room's phone it suddenly sounded like the ringing was coming from the hallway. She went out, opened the door to Room 409. The ringing continued.

She went in, walked a few feet into the room, and came to a stop. She held herself there, poised, waiting. There wasn't another ring. With a smirk and a laugh at herself, Ms. Maxwell turned about and headed back out into the hallway, closing the door behind her.

She turned back and locked it with her key, and that's when the ringing started again. Frowning – and sure that someone down at the front desk was playing a trick on her – she turned back and unlocked the door and threw it open. Immediately Ms. Maxwell was hit with a chill, some kind of cold force.

That's how she described it, as a "force," one that blew back at her. Her eyes went wide, for although nothing about the room had changed, it was as if she'd entered a freezer or meat locker. The temperature had suddenly dropped from the regular 64°F to something more like -10°F.

That's when the ringing started again, startling Ms. Maxwell from her thoughts. She realized she'd been standing there, shocked into inaction by the cold. More than just moments had passed, much more. The phone was ringing again, though, as if a new caller was trying to get through.

At that moment a chill went up Ms. Maxwell's spine and she turned from the room, closed it and locked it and did the same with Room 408 across the hall. She went to some other floors and didn't go back that day.

There were three more incidents that 1932 and then seven in 1933. The next year saw eleven and in 1935 there were thirty-two incidents.

Incidents primarily consisted of the phone ringing, though just like with Ms. Maxwell, if anyone picked up the phone there was nothing on the other end.

Overwhelmingly too the phone rang for maids, and primarily women. Back in the '30s there were only women serving in those roles, but by the 1970s and 1980s men were filling them. The only time the phone has been heard by a man is if he's gay.

This is one of the main reasons why people think the phone is haunted by a woman. Some think it's haunted by a dead maid, since they hear the phone so much, but there's no recorded mention of a maid dying in the hotel. What research has been done on maids that worked at the Cecil and later died shows nothing of relevance – most passed away in old age.

The incidents continued until 1942 when they tapered off. In 1943 and 1944 there were no incidents at all, and then in 1945 there were just two. This has led to the belief that the phone is haunted by a dead soldier, perhaps one that stayed in the hotel before shipping off to Europe in 1917. Research has yet to be done on this front.

The incidents continued in the 1950s and 1960s, though in the early-70s they again tapered off – 1972 was another year that no incidents were recorded.

There have never been any deaths attributed to the phone, it's more an inconvenience than anything. While the cold that Ms. Maxwell experienced has been felt by others on occasion, there's only one incident with it that's worth mentioning.

In 2011 a young woman named Meg Winton stayed at the Cecil, and in Room 408 specifically. We know she heard the phone because she called down to the front desk about it.

They assured her it was nothing, just some faulty wiring from the '30s. The hotel had used that line many times before, and it usually worked, more so because the phone always stopped ringing after a time than because the story was true, which it wasn't – the wiring was fine, always had been.

That day, however, Ms. Winton had her cell phone. She texted her boyfriend in Chicago that she was feeling strange, that the room was getting colder.

There was no reply from him, and we later learned he was playing basketball at the time and away from his phone. Ms. Winton kept up her texts, however.

She reports the appearance of ice in the bathroom, and even the lights of the room dimming slightly off and on. Her last message says how she was going into the bathroom to look.

Meg Winton was never heard from again, and because of a quick response by hotel management, the press didn't get word of it. A financial settlement was reached with the family, the same year the hotel reported a miscellaneous building expense of $15 million. No police report was ever filed.

Whatever happened to Meg Winton is unknown. The "phantom ringing" continues on the third floor of the Cecil, though the staff was instructed in the 1950s to stop referring to it as that. Most sources say it's now simply referred to as "the phone."

Whether you call it "the phone," "phantom ringing," or "the phone that wasn't there," either way, it's clear that something is happening at the Cecil Hotel.

THE END

7. A STAIRWAY TO HELL

The church was large, built of strong wood and cemented at the seams. She showed that wood at her tresses but further up she was all white. There was no competition with the surrounding trees either. Nay, some of them were even taller, allowed to grow. This was a church that allowed the majesty of God to shine through, and overshadow. It was a servant to the Lord, not its master. Those who attended her felt the same.

Her name was Our Heavenly Redeemer's Pentecostal. She'd been built in 1954 and had seen 37 parishioners that first year. By the second she had 48 and as the 60s started it was up to 104.

The numbers grew over the years, new members coming, old members dying off. Few, however, knew the truth.

~~~
~~~

Pastor James Merit stood by the doors, watched the last of the parishioners leave. He waved one last time as they got into their car and started to drive away. It was only after they'd reached the edge of the parking lot that he let his smile falter, then fade altogether. *Finally*, he thought, *another Goddamn Sunday over with.*

James headed back through the large wooden double doors and then down the corridor leading to the nave. It was off from the main chapel area, which could now seat 200 comfortably. Most Sundays they were lucky to get a quarter of that, however. Publicly James blamed the internet, troubled youth, and of course the old fallback, sexuality.

He took in a breath and let it out in a sigh as he passed by the pews, finally reaching the chancel and then the door to the back, the sanctuary area. He opened it, walked down the short hall to another door and opened it. This one let onto a short stairway that went two steps then turned left to go down several more. He started down, his footfalls echoing as he did so.

Below, Smith looked up, then spoke up before James came into view.

"Is that everyone?"

"That's everyone," James said with a nod when he got down the stairs and into the small basement. It was a storeroom, one with boxes piled high, Christmas decorations poking from many. The room wasn't all for show, James knew.

Across that room Smith nodded. He was tall, gray-bearded and wearing a dark suit. James had never seen him before, but he knew the group he was with.

"Good, then let's begin," Smith said. "It's Purim this evening – we need to be ready."

With that he spun around and started to the wall, one that had several boxes stacked against it. He started to pull them out, set them atop one another behind himself. By the third the top of a door appeared on the wall, white and country-home-like, a sharp contrast to the bare cement walls. Smith continued on and a few moments later the door was clear. Without looking back he went to it, opened it. A rush of warmth, heat really, rushed out at him, engulfed James standing several feet back.

Without pausing, Smith headed through the door, then down the stairs that were past the threshold's landing. James moved to follow.

~~~

Billy Myers poked his head up from behind the pew, looked around, then rose up. The coast was clear – no one had seen him.

He'd stayed behind in the empty church after the mass, though no one had known it. He'd told his aunt that he'd walk home after the service, skipping her usual round of coffee and chit-chatting. She'd been fine with that, hadn't suspected for a second on what he'd really meant to do.

Billy stared ahead. There was the hallway Pastor James had gone down. That's where the stairway supposedly was.

Billy gritted his teeth. He wasn't sure if the stories were true. Ed Mortenson at school said they were, said he'd seen the stairway himself. Kyle Connors had said that was bullshit. After that no one had said anything because Ed had hit Kyle in the mouth and a fight broke out and then the playground assistant was called and both were carted off to Principle Dickers' office.

Billy sighed. He didn't think Kyle was telling the truth anyways. Now he'd have the chance to find out.

Moving forward, Billy headed for the hallway.

~~~

What the hell is he doing?

Devan's brows furrowed as he stared ahead, stared at the young boy moving toward the back hallway behind the chancel.

Damn kids, he thought as he started forward, slowly for his left leg was lame, had been ever since…

Devan took in a deep breath, let it out slowly. He didn't want to think on that day. It was the reason he was at Our Heavenly Redeemers, had been for years. No one knew it of course, no one knew the pre-teen was living there, cleaning the place, seeing to its 'needs.'

He shook his head, shook the thoughts away. Whatever that little bastard was doing was not good and Devan meant to stop him.

~~~
~~~

Pastor James headed down the staircase, which was only twenty or so steps. He'd never counted, for he'd only been down it a few times and each of them he'd been far too afraid to count his steps.

That fear was coming on now for the bottom of the staircase was getting closer. James could see it, could see the way the landing gave way to stone, but not just any stone, an unearthly stone, the kind that belonged in only one place – Hell.

Another few steps and James was there, on that landing. He gulped as the sight unfolded before him. There past the landing was what he could only describe as an abyss. It was dark and empty, stretching far up above him, like some empty section of outer space that'd been robbed of its stars. Slowly, almost imperceptibly, the emptiness gave way to walls. It was so faint you could barely notice where it started but then all of a sudden there were these walls of jagged and distorted rock. They moved downward, oh so far downward, to an area James's eyes didn't want to take in.

Past the walkway the rocks appeared but the stairs kept on, that same ugly 1950s tiling of white with green flecks and a faint trace of gold glitter. They hung there unnaturally, out in that empty space, heading downward to the faint orangish glow that was the only trace there was anything below.

Ahead of him Smith looked back, narrowed his eyes in a scowl, one that said, 'hurry up.' The man was already a good two dozen steps ahead of him, suspended out in that nothingness. He showed no fear, something James couldn't say.

What scared him more was not going, however, so he kept on.

~~~

Billy's eyes went wide as he opened the door, felt the rush of hot and unnatural air. *It was true, it was all true – Our Heavenly Redeemers did have a stairway to Hell!*

Billy smiled, but a moment later it slipped from his face. He could leave now, could tell Kyle and Ed at school. Yet something was telling him that wasn't enough, something was telling him he had to *see* it too.

Frowning, and not quite sure why he was doing so, Billy stepped forward, started down the steps.
~~~

~~~

God, the wailing was awful! James put his hands to his ears, tried to drown it out as best as he could.

Ahead of him Smith kept on, seemingly unaffected by the noise. And what a noise it was. To James it seemed the desperate and depressed pleas of those damned for all eternity. It was, he knew, that's exactly what it was. All around him it rose up, and even now, dozens of steps down the stairway, he could begin to see some of them, there against the rocks further below, writhing in their chains.

The sight repulsed him, yet onward he continued.

~~~

Billy couldn't believe the noise, the unending cries of pity and agony coming up from the hell hole. That's what he thought of it as, a 'hell hole.' Even now he was getting a sight of something further down, past Pastor James and the man that was walking ahead of him. Why he was still continuing on he had no idea.

After leaving the landing and stepping out on the rocky ground that surround the steps hanging in a void of nothingness, Billy had moved forward. He'd felt compelled, though why or for what reason he couldn't have said.

Those thoughts were at the forefront of his mind suddenly, and he stopped, stopped his foot from moving forward, stopped it from stepping down on the next step.

I've got to go, he thought, *I've got to get out of here.*

He started to turn and–

KA-KAW!

Billy put his arms up just at the last moment, just before the 'bird' flew right at him. It wasn't a bird though, he'd known that right away. Birds didn't have long tails with barbed hooks at the end, birds didn't emit such ungodly calls.

"Ah!" he said, croaked really, and just before he fell down on to the stairway.

Looking up he saw the 'bird' far above him, circling about, looking to come back down again. He noticed something else too, however – the silence. All around him the wailing had stopped. More than that, however, he could tell that the attention of the place was fixed upon him, if that was at all possible. But then Billy knew that in this strange place, all manner of impossibilities were not only possible, but likely.

Gulping, he rose up, turned and started back up the steps. He was slow at first, taking one at a time as he glanced back up at the 'bird' overhead, some kind of demon serpent pterodactyl thing, he saw. He began taking the stairs two at a time, moving higher, higher, closer and closer to the…

Billy stopped, bounded down on a step not more than ten steps from the landing. There, in the doorway and still within the small stairwell hallway that left the basement storeroom, was a big kid, someone that'd probably be in 5th or 6th grade at school…if Billy had ever seen him at school, which he hadn't.

Billy was glad for that, for that unknown face took on a twisted smile. That's when he knew what was going to happen.

"No!" he shouted, then started to bound up the steps again, but it was too late. Ahead of him, Devan closed the door.

SLAM!

~~~

James looked up, looked back up the stairway. There, more than a hundred steps above, the door had closed. Worse, there was one of the church boys…Billy Myers by the look of him…and just then starting to pound on the door.

BOOM! BOOM! BOOM!

The sound echoed and reverberated down to them. James turned back, saw Smith now stopped and looking back as well.

Shit, James thought. The last thing he wanted was to look foolish in front of Smith. He turned, started back up the steps.

~~~

Billy ran on and reached the door. Immediately his fists began slamming down. It was no use – the door would not budge. Frantic, he looked about.

There!

His eyes shot onto a stone lying loose on the landing. He jumped down, grabbed it.

~~~

BANG!

The sound flew out over the abyss, drowned out the usual wailing. James looked up, saw Billy pull his fist back and slam the stone down again.

"No!" James yelled.

"You fool!" a voice called out behind him, and James spun around. Smith was right there. "You said the church was empty!"

"I…I…" James managed, shocked by Smith staring down at him. His eyes went wide as Smith sneered then brought his fist up. He slammed it into James's stomach, sending the pastor down. Next he kicked, and hard. Suddenly James was flying down, flying into the abyss. He started to scream.

KA-KAW-KAW!

"Aaahhh!"

James screamed as one of the 'birds' ripped into his crotch, ripped into it and ripped it away, his backside as well. He was still screaming, his upper body falling this way and his legs falling that way, at least until death took him.

~~~

Billy's fist slammed down again, and this time the stone splintered the wood. His eyes went wide, he smiled, and brought his fist back and slammed it down again. The wood splintered some more, this time sending splinters flying off to land on the stone steps.

~~~

Devan frowned and turned back. The door had shuddered then–

Devan's eyes went wide. The door had splintered. The damn kid was pounding away at it with something. He moved back down the stairs toward it.

~~~

Billy kept on hammering away at the door with the stone. He had it breaking now, had a crack large enough to see through. He brought it back again and again and–"

Fingers! Billy thought, a moment before the stone slammed down on them.

~~~

"Yow!" Devan shouted as the stone hit his fingers. He pulled them back quickly, regretted his decision to stick them out. Why he'd been compelled to do so he had no idea. He frowned, reached down to his pocket and the pocketknife there. He pulled it out, got the blade up, and smiled.

~~~

Smith raced up the stairs, eager to kill the child that was slamming on the portal. His master would not like that portal destroyed, would not like it one bit.

He was just a few stairs away now. He smiled, enjoying the thought of his fingers digging into the child's eye-sockets.

~~~

The hole in the door was large enough now, Billy saw, he could reach his hand through and unlock it! Just then, however, he heard the footsteps, heard the pounding of feet on the stone steps.

Oh no, he thought, and dodged out of the way.

~~~

Oh no, Smith thought, just after he'd entered his dive into the child…or at least where the child had been. Instead, his head went forward, right toward the hole the child had torn into the portal.

~~~

Devan smiled as he stabbed forward, then frowned. Instead of the kid's hand coming in with a rock it was some man's head. His knife went right into the man's eye and then forward more, right up to his
~~~

fingers.

Devan's eyes went wide and he croaked and dropped the knife, fled up the stairs. One foot stepped down on his untied shoelaces and he fell forward, struck one stair with his forehead. The pointed edge dug in and sliced an inch into his brain, killing him instantly.

~~~

Billy stared at the man sitting there hunched over, his head stuck in the small hole in the door. He was dead, Billy knew that for sure because he wasn't moving. While the wailing had stopped, the silence had not. Now it seemed as though a great feeling of satisfaction, triumph even, had shot up at him from the depths below.

He got up and kicked at the man, toppling him over onto the stone landing. It was then that he saw the handle-end of a pocketknife sticking from the man's eye. He gave one last look of horror out at the vast open abyss behind him then stuck his arm through the hole in the door and unlocked it from the other side.

The door opened and he saw the dead 5th or 6th grader, his forehead sliced open by one of the steps. With a shudder he started up. Behind him the door hung open for a minute, then with one giant gush of air, the bodies of the two were sucked out, sucked into the abyss and the waiting maws of the 'birds'.

~~~

Billy ran for all he was worth, ran up the stairs and through the church and to its front doors. He ran and yelled for help and tore right into the parking lot.

There ahead of him was a car, one that was pulling into the parking lot, up to the front doors in fact.

"Help, help!" Billy yelled, rushing up to it.

The car stopped, a man got out.

"Mr., you gotta—"

"Easy, easy," the man said, still wearing his Sunday church suit, still in a good mood. "What's going on here? I came back to speak with Pastor James for a moment."

"Pastor James is dead," Billy blurted out, "one of the 'birds' got him."

The man narrowed his eyes at Billy but said nothing. When the boy looked up at him, tears in his eyes, he nodded.

"C'mon, get in the car – I'll get you to the police."

"Ah, thanks, Mr.," Billy said, and started toward the backdoor of the car that the man was just opening. "If we can get–"

Billy stopped, looked down.

"It's alright," the man said, pulling the knife back, its blade bloodied from Billy's kidney, "just sit down, it's alright."

"Alright," Billy said, already feeling sleepy. He got into the car, closed his eyes, and knew no more.

THE END

8. THE POND IN SETTER'S WOOD

When did the evil first come?

No one really knew, least of all Conner Douglas.

He was just 14, after all, not even in high school yet. He would be next year, which was really just a couple months. Yep, it was summer in Michigan's Upper Peninsula, though summer was almost over. Conner and his friends discussed that while sitting by Gooseneck Creek.

"There ain't nothin' *to* do!" James nearly shouts, though it comes out as more of a sigh, a depressed one at that.

James was the outspoken leader of the group, though he'd only achieved that position by being more bully than leader. His hair was a wavy brown, his eyes the same color, and his face small and compact with a straight nose and long cheekbones that'd have the girls all over him in another year or two.

"Yeah, no *duh!*" Mike says, rolling his eyes.

Mike was the brains of the bunch, at least if you went by his report cards. All A's except for that damn B+ in shop class. God, he hated thinking about that *and* that damn Mr. Reynolds and his hand with one finger missing from some classroom accident back in the 80s. *Remember, safety* first*, not second,* he'd always say, walking around and holding that half-finger up before putting up a second, longer one beside it.

Mike rolled his eyes again as the image of that finger came into his mind. He had short, black hair that hung straight, and despite having just turned 15, he was showing the first faint traces of a mustache on that upper lip of his.

"What, you suddenly *forget* you've spent your whole life in Houghton?" Spitty says, to laughs from Conner and Mike, but a raised fist and mock gesture from James.

Spitty's real name was Sinclair, but everyone called him Spitty because of the time in 3rd grade when the boys tricked him into drinking from the teacher's bourbon-laced coffee. He'd spent the next 15 minutes spitting it up, much to the enjoyment of the class, though not to the teacher's. She hadn't been around much longer after that, but the boys had.

Fifteen years was a long time to spend in Houghton, a backwater town of 8,000 located four hours north of Green Bay. It might as well have been a million miles, for all the good it did the town. Ever since 2008 businesses had been closing, and nothing had been coming in to replace them. The real blow came in 2011 when the copper mine closed its doors. Three months later the brass fitting plant closed up shop, ending a 131-year tradition of keeping it local. Now the parts would be made in Mexico.

Trump would change all that, of course – their daddies all said so. Well, James's, Mike's and Spitty's did. Conner hadn't had a dad since his had walked out on his mom when he was just 2. The revolving door of alcoholic and drug-addicted substitute dads that took up the part for a time didn't much discuss politics, or at least Conner didn't hear them. But then they'd be gone after his mom finally got tired of the inevitable beatings, the process starting over once again. Conner wondered if the current father-figure in his life – a real piece of work named Henry – was still beating his mom or passed out already. It was past 3 in the afternoon, after all. The thought made Conner want to go anywhere but home, and he said so.

"I got an idea of where we can go," he says.

"Yeah, where?" Mike replies.

"The pond in Setter's Wood."

Silence meets that pronouncement, silence and wide-eyed looks. *Was Henry layin' into Conner now too and not just his mom?* the boys think.

The thing was…the pond in Setter's Wood was haunted. Everyone knew it. No one talked about it. It'd been that way for years, decades…centuries even. And it was *still* haunted. They all remembered the stories from two years ago when that high schooler from Dollar Bay was found dead there, just splayed out there right beside the pond. No cause of death was ever determined.

It wasn't the first death, that was for sure.

They'd all heard the stories. Back in the 1920s a woman – fraught with despair over the thought that the man she loved didn't love her in return – rushed into Setter's Wood and found herself at a pond there. Feeling all was lost, she flung herself into the water and drowned.

The man she thought hadn't loved her mounted a search and they found the body the next day. The mausoleum he built for her in Forest Hill Cemetery was still the largest in the state. He joined her in it three years later, at the ripe old age of 32. Most said it was a broken heart that'd killed him. Others said it was a heart attack after seeing his former love come up out of the pond for him. His body had been found next to the same pond she'd killed herself at, after all, though that wasn't that unusual. He'd had a stone bench installed at the pond and was known to sit on it for hours at a time, just staring into the waters.

Some said it was the bench that was haunted, and not the pond. Infused with some kind of witch-enhanced stone or cement, it exuded dark auras and instilled nasty thoughts in all those that sat upon it. Others said it wasn't the pond at all, but the forest around it. Stories of old Indian sacrifices and burial grounds usually came up as explanation. Then there was the talk of secret portals, extra dimensions, even UFOs or Bigfoots. In the end, however, no on really knew what the cause of the deaths was. So far there'd been more than forty over the years.

"I'll go," Conner says finally, breaking the silence.

"*What?*" Spitty says, his face screwing up in shock and concern and disbelief, while beside him James smiles and claps Conner on the back, letting out a, "That's my man!" as he does so. All eyes then go to Mike.

"Well?" James says to him.

Mike moves his jaw from side to side for a few moments, then gives a shrug and says, "aw, fuck it – let's go."

There were a lot of, "But…but…but's" from Spitty, but the other three were already laughing and joking as they started to walk. They kept it up the two miles to Setter's Wood, the better to push down their fear, which of course none of them would admit they felt. The talking died down, however, as the boys got deeper into the Wood, and then ceased altogether as they got closer to the pond.

None of them had been there before, but they knew they were on the right path. From time to time they'd see a 'Danger' sign pounded to a tree, or maybe a 'Keep Out.' One time they saw a sign with no words, just a yellow yield-style sign with a skull and crossbones in red over it. That one had stopped Spitty in his tracks.

"Guys, I'm goin' home."

"To cry to momma?" James had shot back, chuckling.

"C'mon, man…it's just a little farther," Mike had said.

Conner had said nothing, just paused for a moment before continuing on. Soon the others were following behind him once again. In all it took them nearly an hour of walking into Setter's Wood before they came to the pond, and they nearly missed the thing entirely, so small was it.

"God, I've seen parking lot puddles bigger than that!" Mike says when they're all standing there.

"And how 'bout that stupid bench, huh?" James says, pointing over at it and laughing. It looks like a child's bench almost, so small is it.

"Yeah, but how about that pond, huh?" Conner says, and begins moving toward it.

A few broken branches stuck up around the pond's edges, while last year's dead grass still clung to what new growth could push up around the water. There were a few healthy-looking pine trees a ways back, but most of the trees that were closest to the pond – white ash, birch, and ironwoods – had spindly branches with no leaves, branches that seemed almost like skeletal claws just waiting for some young boys to grab and pull into the pond.

The summer sun seemed to fade away as the boys stood there, and it wasn't just that it'd gone behind a cloud. A mist was appearing, they would swear, a kind of fog that was slowly moving in from all sides. An evil was moving in on them too.

"Guys, I don't like the feel of this place," Spitty says.

"Just…just…look at the water," James says, his usual snide tone gone and replaced by something…else. He too begins walking toward the pond.

Mike rolls his eyes at the two and turns back to look at Spitty, who's slowly backing away. "It's alright," he says, "let's just…"

His voice trails-off as some strange feeling takes hold of him. He looks back at Conner and James, suddenly feeling that they've made a very bad mistake.

The pond is seemingly pulling the boys toward it. Conner is staring at it intently, looking deeply into its shallow water as he slowly walks toward it. Behind him, James's face is a mask of struggle, one part of him wanting to go toward the pond, another wanting to pull away from it. Still, for every step back he takes he goes another two forward.

Mike was doing the best to stay away, looking over his shoulder at Spitty backing off while glancing forward at the other two, and saying, "Guys, don't do this…don't do this…" over and over, perhaps more to himself than the others.

Spitty was the furthest back, perhaps thirty yards from the water's edge. He saw what was happening to Conner and James, and also how Mike was beginning to struggle. He wants to turn and run…but just can't seem to.

Conner is at the edge of the pond now, and beginning to kneel down as if to look at something in the water. What he doesn't see – but what Mike and Spitty both see clearly – are wispy tentacles rising up from the center of the pond. They're not real; he can see that right away. They're more smoke than substance, almost like they were formed out of the same fog-like mist that was closing in on them from the trees.

"Conner, Conner!" Mike shouts, but it does no good. Conner doesn't hear him, and it's as if James doesn't see what's going on either. He's now just feet from the edge of the pond, and in a few moments he'll be there, probably to kneel down beside Conner and look at whatever it is they're looking at.

Further back, Spitty had seen enough. Without a word he turns and starts running back into the trees.

"Spitty…Spitty!" Mike calls after him, still turning his head back and forth to look from him to the other two. Then Spitty is gone, swallowed up by the trees and out of sight. "Shit," Mike mutters, and turns his attention fully back to Conner and James. He can't believe what he sees. The tentacles are reaching for his friends!

Mike struggles, wants to call out again, but can't seem to make his mouth work. He also can't seem to make his legs work, though they're moving just fine…moving him closer to the pond, that is. The fog and mist are getting closer too. Already Mike can't even see the trees on the other side of the pond, just the water now.

And then it happens. Those tentacles of white mist or smoke or whatever they are lunge forward, latch onto Conner as he's looking down…but don't grab 'him.' Instead Conner's body stays right there, but it's as if his…*soul*…is grabbed.

Mike watches wide-eyed as the tentacles seem to stick onto a white corporeal form of Conner and pull it from his body, then right down into the pond. James – or at least his body – collapses beside the pond, a pale, ghost-like look to it.

A moment later another tentacle shoots forth, this one at James. The same thing happens – that white corporeal form is pulled from James's body and then James collapses, dead…Mike knows he's dead.

He knows he'll be dead soon too. His feet continue to carry him forward, closer to the pond, which is now just a few feet away. Tears begin to come to Mike's eyes, but he can't stop himself from moving. Then the white mist closes in all around him and he's at the pond, and then looking down into it.

His eyes go wide at what he sees, but only for a moment. Then something cold touches him, and all the warmth seems to flood out of him. He never feels his body collapse to the ground beside his two friends.

Three hours later Spitty was back, this time with the police and sheriff's deputies and even some firemen.

They found Conner, James and Mike laying there dead beside the pond, no sign of foul play and no sign that they'd even *been* in the water, let alone drowned in it. When Spitty tells them of the mist and the tentacles the first responders cast weary glances at one another, but no one jokes. They'd heard similar before and knew what the coroner would make of it.

"Can't find a cause of death to save my life," he'd say, the same thing he'd been saying since he took the job back in '74.

The next day the *Mining Gazette* runs the story, saying that the pond in Setter's Wood has claimed yet more lives. That puts the grand total up to forty-seven since the deaths had started nearly one hundred years before. And there'd likely be more, the article had finished…a lot more.

THE END

9. LAST STOP ON THE UNDERGROUND RAILROAD

The Waterbury House had been standing in town since 1826.

It was named for the Waterbury Family, specifically Joel and Eliza. They'd built the place in the years after the Panic of 1819, trying to get a bit of security for themselves and what they hoped would be a growing family. Their hopes came true, and within a few years the house was full of laughing children.

But Joel and Eliza weren't the sort to just raise their own kids and be happy. No, they wanted to help the world, too. The best way to do that was to fight slavery. So they did a little carpentry work around the house and soon had some removable floorboards, hiding spaces in the attic, and a false wall in one room. A carriage ride to Richmond a few weeks later saw Joel meeting with the right contact. A week after that they had their first runaway, a slave named Ned that came all the way from Georgia. They managed to get him up to Vermont after a stay of a few days at their home. It was their first 'trip' on the Underground Railroad, as the system to free escaped slaves to the North was called, and from that point on they were hooked.

That'd been in 1831, and for the next quarter-century, Joel and Eliza helped usher escaped slaves from the South to their freedom in the North. Their kids helped once they were grown and of age, specifically their youngest, Todd. There were already plans in place for him to inherit the house over his siblings, solely because he intended to continue their 'stop' on the Railroad.

Of course, much of the talk around the country by then was that the nation wouldn't have slavery for much longer…if it even managed to remain a nation. Talk of war was on the horizon, and Todd and Eliza had no idea how that would affect their operation. They hoped that it would end it…and in a good way, the way that would come if the nation finally shrugged off the shackles and chains of the oppressed. They also knew it could end poorly, with the nation instituting slavery in every state. Then there'd be no place for the slaves to run.

The two put that thought out of their mind and continued with their work, Todd helping more and more as the years passed. It seemed more and more slaves were trying to get North as talk of war grew. One of them was named Hobbs, and he first came to the Waterbury house in April 1859.

Hobbs was from South Carolina, and he didn't come to the Waterbury House alone – he came with a spirit.

Joel made it a point to get to know the runaways as best he could. He did this not through prodding or cajoling, but simply through kindness. He'd fetch them water, bring them food, mend their tattered clothing. All came to him tight-lipped, but after his niceties, most talked. They talked of the places they were running from and the places they were running to. Most often, neither had a name. Where they were going were more dreams than realities, where they'd been were the stuff of nightmares.

Tales of whippings and beatings and rape and murder were common. Joel heard more, though. Men routinely told of being sold and sent away from their wives and children, never to see them again. He heard women tell of their children killed in front of them for the most minor of 'infractions.' The youngest of the slaves always told tales of abuse, most often sexual.

Hobbs was different. He didn't talk at all. There were quite a few over the years that were like that, so broken and tortured that they couldn't trust anyone, least of all themselves. They just wanted to get away. Always north…wherever that may have led.

But Hobbs didn't even let on to that much. Joel brought him water and sewed the tears in his tattered pants, but the slave didn't say a word. He seemed indifferent to it all, like he didn't care if he made it to freedom or not.

"He's an odd one," Joel said to Eliza after he'd wished Hobbs well for the night, leaving him a lantern to help him see. The two felt confident enough in the late season and the lack of travelers on the road to keep Hobbs in the shed out back for the night. By morning he'd be gone, off in the back of Russell's cart, a friendly trader that came through to head north, bringing the escaped slaves to some other sympathetic family.

The old couple turned in for the night, their minds more focused on the next day's chores than the escaped slave sleeping out back. But well past midnight, something awoke the two of them.

"Did you…hear that?" Eliza said, rubbing the sleep from her eyes.

Beside her, Joel nodded in the darkness. *Hear* wasn't really the word, he thought to himself as he threw his legs over the bed, more like *felt*.

He went to the window and looked out, expecting storm clouds. Instead, there were lights coming from the shed out back…the shed that housed Hobbs. They were strange lights, too…fading in and out and pulsing and throbbing. They were reds and purples and now and again, a flash of yellow, as if lightning was swirling around amidst the jumble.

"What is it?" Eliza asked from the bed.

"I…I…don't know," Joel replied in a shaky voice. He turned back to look at his wife, but when he saw she was about to get up and look out the window as well, he changed his tone. "It…it's probably nothing, but I'll go have a look."

In the bed, Eliza relaxed back. Joel grabbed the lantern and left the room. He was soon down the stairs and through the back door. The shed was just a few dozen feet away, the lights still emanating from it.

Mustering every bit of courage he could, Joel walked to it. Reaching it, he pressed his face to the dirty glass of the window and peered in. What he saw shocked him.

Shadows danced on the walls, illuminated by the smallest of fires burning on the floor in the center of the shed. It was a single flame, lit by dead leaves and hair and some small twigs…but it seemed like a mighty conflagration, the way it was giving off light. The light caused the shadows, though where they were coming from – or what was making them – Joel hadn't a clue. He could pick out at least four shadowy figures, all humanlike, but two had hoofs instead of feet and one had large horns growing from its head. And even in shadow form, the things had eyes…red eyes, burning with deadly curiosity and mischief. In the center of the shed was Hobbs, his shirt off and sweat pouring down him. He was chanting in some foreign tongue, just the whites of his eyes showing.

Then the chanting stopped and those eyes turned to the window, locked onto Joel, into him and through him.

Joel's own eyes went wide, and he staggered back from the window, falling down in the process. The next thing he knew he was up and running back to the house. Behind him, he heard deep-throated laughter…the kind no human could make.

Joel didn't get another wink of sleep that night. When morning came and Eliza began to stir, he held her down in bed, though not explaining why. They stayed that way for the first few hours of daylight, until they heard the sounds of Russell coming, their northern contact on the Railroad.

The two waited until the sounds of Russell taking Hobbs away had faded…then waited some more. Joel wouldn't explain anything to Eliza, of what he saw or heard, of what he thought Hobbs was. It wasn't until their son Todd came later that day that and found them still in bed that Joel allowed the two of them to get up. He wouldn't speak of what he saw in the night, just insisted he'd never take another runaway so long as he lived.

Hobbs would prove to be the last slave they helped escape to the north.

THE END

10. THE GHOST IN THE BASEMENT

I work nights in a bar. It's a part-time gig. It has been for the past five years.

It's a working-class joint, known for its stiff pours. Two pool tables in the back, casino machines in front, and a long bar to get your drink on. It's a lively place on the weekends, with loud music blaring from the jukebox and people singing and dancing along to it.

It's built at the old part of downtown, the first section that was built-up in the 1880s when the train came through. The building's been there since the early 1910s. The bar was added in the 1930s. A restaurant side came in the 2010s. It's just the ground floor with the bar and then the basement, where we keep the walk-in cooler, some office desks, supplies and other odds-and-ends.

Oh…and the ghost.

I've never seen it or heard from it, myself, and I spend a lot of time in the basement. It's really just a rumor more than anything. There are stories from staff, but nothing substantial has ever happened.

Most of the stories date to before the time I worked there. There was the night everyone was closing up and one of the light bulbs started flickering, like it was about to burn-out.

"Stop that damn light flickering, ghost!" one of the bouncers shouted out, eliciting laughter from his coworkers. But then the light stopped flickering and remained steady. People were freaked out.

You certainly get an eerie sensation when you go downstairs, especially on the slower nights when there's not as many people upstairs. A cold chill runs through you as you go about your tasks, like someone…or *something*…is watching you. Other times an overwhelming sense of dread came over you, filling your body and diluting your mind.

When discussed with some of the staff that'd been there the longest, they chalked it up to the ghost. No one ever had an explanation for what the ghost was, where it came from, what it was doing there, or what it wanted.

It just *was*.

So business went on as usual, customers got drunk, staff made bank, and the seasons went from one to the next.

Then one summer it happened.

It was busy, the first major travel year after the pandemic. It seemed every damn tourist and their mother was in town, and many wanted to blow off the steam of travelling by visiting a good bar and having a few stiff pours. The cooks worked their asses off during the days while the bartenders bustled by night. Money flowed. Anxieties increased. Most drank to ease the workload.

One was Reggie. He drank a lot, but was in good spirits. Everyone knew he had problems, but he managed. The kitchen was so hard-pressed for workers that they hired him, and he did well. Each night he spent his tips on beers and the pool table.

Thankfully he didn't drive. He had a good bike but got into a bad wreck one night riding home drunk. If it wasn't for his helmet, he'd have killed himself. The bike was totaled. Somehow, Reggie got a new one a few weeks later. It was better than the last, and more expensive. Reggie didn't trust leaving the bike outside locked up, so he'd put it down in the basement while working his shifts, often leaving it there while he drank in the evenings and typically to closing time around 2 AM.

And my God, was he a handful! He was a great person…but when he drank too much he'd get ornery and pushy and it was often his way or the highway.

That's how it was the night he came storming back a half hour till close, drunk and likely kicked out of another bar. We refused to serve him, so he declared that he'd be going downstairs to get his bike to ride home.

Fine, we thought, *just go and get out of here so we can close up.*

And close up we did. We poured the last few for people, got

everything cleaned and washed-up, closed the till, counted the tips, and locked the doors.

We didn't know that Reggie was still downstairs.

Usually I stock beer at the end of the night, but I'd already done that an hour before close and didn't need to redo it. So I didn't go over by the walk-in beer cooler, where Reggie usually kept his bike. If I had, I would have seen the bike and thought…*Oh, maybe he* didn't *go home after all. Maybe he's still here.*

But I didn't think that. Instead I drove home and went to bed.

The opening bartender found Reggie the next day. He was in the walk-in cooler with the beer, a can of PBR still in his hand, just a few sips taken from it.

Reggie was nearly frozen, but the later autopsy would prove he didn't die that way. Instead, it was fear that killed him. He saw or heard something that gave him such a fright that stopped his heart cold.

But not before it turned every hair on his head a blinding white color.

No one knew how it happened, and management wanted to keep it hush-hush. They didn't want word to get out that someone died in the building – it'd kill sales.

It was just another story that was blamed on the ghost in the basement.

THE END

11. ON THE ROCKS

Captain Hern didn't like the look of it, not one bit. He scowled once again as he lowered the looking glass from his eye. It'd be rough…maybe too rough.

The cause of the captain's concern was the opening to Whitefish Bay, the way he'd have to take if he were to get off the lake successfully. It was the most-used route to get on and off Lake Superior, the largest of the country's five Great Lakes. It was also called the "Graveyard of the Great Lakes." Numerous shipwrecks lay in the murky depths below them.

Thankfully, there was the light to guide them. It was Whitefish Point Light, built way back in 1847 but not lit until two years later. She wasn't the first light on the lake, but she now had the distinction of the oldest still standing. Well, most of her. She'd been rebuilt in 1861 with an iron skeletal steel framework that was meant to relieve the stress from the constant winds. Originally the light had Lewis lamps inside but those were swapped-out with Fresnel lenses a short time later, increasing the light's range by miles. A hundred years would go by before the DCB-224 aero beacon was installed in their place, allowing the light to be seen 30 miles out on the lake. The keepers operated the new light for just three years before Whitefish Point Light went automated.

"Watch out!" Hern cried, but it was too late. The boom came loose and swung across the deck in a flash. Hern saw three men hit and swept overboard immediately. Others cried that the boom was going to come back, to jump out of the way or get down. Some managed to, but another two men were hit and knocked into the sea as well.

Another large wave hit them, this time from the port side. Somehow, the ship must've gotten turned about for that to occur, but Hern had no idea how that'd happened. Then another crash came and with it the sound of wood splintering on rock. More yelling from below, more shouts of water rushing in. With each passing second, hope fled from Captain Hern.

There was nothing else to do. Hern turned and looked for Peter, his first mate. He was there behind him, taking in the carnage all around.

"Give the signal to abandon ship," Hern said. "Help get as many men as you can into the lifeboats."

"And you, Captain?" Peter managed in a stammering voice.

"Don't worry about me," Hern said, though he had no intention of leaving his ship. He turned to look back at the boom, hoping he could somehow do something for it, somehow right his ship.

BOOM!

Another crash came, this one shaking the whole ship something fierce, much more than the others had. The ship began to come apart, and Hern was thrown. His head hit something, and he went out cold.

<center>~~~</center>

"Captain…Captain…"

Hern's eye's fluttered at the sound. It took a few moments, but his vision cleared. He saw Peter staring down at him, and behind were a few other men.

"We thought you were gone, sir," Peter says, relief in his voice.

"The ship," Hern manages, but watches as Peter shakes his head.

"Gone, sir, and most everything and everyone with her. We figure we're the only ones left."

Hern sighed. There was nothing left for them to do then but get up to the light and get inside, out of the weather. Relaying that to Peter, his first mate agreed and soon had the men together. They got the captain to his feet and were soon moving through the pelting rain to the light far up on the rocks. The going was rough, each step misery in the elements.

"Just a bit more," Hern said after they'd been moving for a time, more under his breath and to himself than the others. The cold and tiredness was creeping into his bones, making each step a labor. And then they were there. The rocky path gave way to one of gravel. Looking up, Hern saw they'd made it up the bluff. The lush green lawn of the light's yard stretched before them. Just a hundred feet away was the lighthouse, its kitchen lights on, the sounds of merriment coming from within.

"C'mon, boys! We're almost there," came the shout from behind. Hern didn't have to turn to know that Peter was smiling as he said it. A weight seemed to be taken from Hern's shoulders, and he felt the tension lift from the men behind him.

They continued on, the storm raging around them and the rain coming down as hard as ever. Gravel crunched beneath their boots as they took the last few steps to the lighthouse's front door. The faint sound of music floated to them over the sounds of the storm, fiddles and flute. Captain Hern was the first to reach it and, after a look back at his men and a nod, he raised his hand up and rapped strongly upon the door.

For a moment – just a moment – the sounds of music and merriment coming from within died away. Then they started up again. There was no sound of someone approaching the door, however. Hern frowned and furrowed his brow, brought his fist up to knock again, but then lowered it just as quickly. Instead he brought his hand to the doorknob, clutched it, and ever so slowly turned it. The door began to open before him.

Without looking back at his men, Hern pushed the door open further, revealing the inside of the lighthouse. They were looking into the common room, two tables and chairs all around, a large fire burning, and men sitting and standing all about, each with a drink in their hand. None seemed to take note of the drenched and bedraggled men standing on their doorstep. Hern was about to call out to them…but something stopped him. It was then that he noticed the pallor of the men, the tone of their skin. Each seemed…white…if you wanted to call it that. They had a paleness to them, not like a sickness *per se* – they were all laughing and carousing and drinking, so that wasn't it – but more like what you'd see on a…

That's when it hit Hern like a ton of bricks. The men before him didn't look normal because they *weren't* normal. No…he knew it then with all certainty – these men were dead. And upon that thought, it was as if the energy in the room shifted and the 'men' standing about seemed to notice the new arrivals for the first time. The music ceased, though for the first time, Hern realized that no one was playing any instruments, and there didn't seem to be a record player anywhere. Before he could voice his concerns, however, one of the pale men stepped forward.

"We've been expecting you," he said with a toothy smile, many more gaps showing than teeth.

Hern narrowed his eyes, was about to respond, but stopped himself. The man before him was wearing the garb of a sailor…but the clothes were from another time, another era. They were at least a hundred years old, perhaps more. Hern turned his gaze to some of the others. Many were dressed similarly, with old-fashioned clothes, breaches, shoes with buckles…just nothing modern.

As if sensing his growing awareness, the man in front of him smiled, and as he did so, the music started up again. The men in the room turned back to what they were doing, mainly talking and laughing and drinking.

"Captain…" Peter said from behind. "These men…are they…"

Dead, Hern thought to himself, finishing Peter's thought, *as are we.*

They didn't make it though the wreck, Hern realized then. No one had. They were ghosts, just as these men drinking and carousing were. The lake had finally claimed them.

Hern shrugged and made his way to the table with the liquor. There was nothing to do now but drink life's worries away.

"That's the spirit!" the strange man-ghost said, as if reading Hern's thoughts.

THE END

12. LOCKER 332

"*Oof!*" Clayton went as he hit the floor, most of the air rushing from his lungs. Somehow, he was able to notice that the bell rang, and just the moment he hit. And of course, he heard Colton's final taunt, too:

"Stay down, ya geeky fuck!"

Discretion being the better part of valor, Clayton stayed down. All around him, the other students began filtering away to whatever class they had next, whatever room would hold them for the next fifty minutes. Then Period One would be over, the hallway rush would start again, and they'd all be off to Period Two. *God*, Clayton thought…*I hate high school!*

Most of the other students were gone by the time he picked himself up off the hard, tile floor. Thankfully his bag hadn't come open, so he quickly grabbed it and then dashed off to what he'd been trying to do before he ran into the star of the football team in the first place – get to his locker.

Good ol' locker #456, with the cool lock combo of 16-22-0. Clayton had been using that same locker and that same combination lock since his freshman year. *Three years already*, Clayton thought as he rounded another corner in the hallway. He wasn't moving that fast anymore – *moving faster ain't gonna make me any less tardy* – so he had lots of time to think. High school was about as he'd expected it to be, about as he'd heard it would. Mostly, it was the same as middle school was, just harder academically and worse in just about every other way.

Let's face it – Clayton was a geek. He liked comics, computers, D&D, books, and math. He didn't like sports, working out, drinking, smoking pot, or making fun of 'losers.' The latter was what he and many other high schoolers were called by the jocks on the football and basketball and wrestling teams, and most of their girlfriends, too.

That was another thing – Clayton might have been a 'geeky fuck,' as Colton liked to call him, but God, did he have the hots for the girls! Big, small, hot, ugly, young or old…Clayton didn't give a fuck, he just *wanted* to *fuck!* But like most high school geeks, he was only fucking his hand, typically three to four times a day. Colton's girlfriend was often the fantasy of encouragement during many of those jerk-off sessions.

Another turn in the hallway brought Clayton's thoughts to a crashing end. There, in the stretch of hallway between Rooms 116 and 118, was where his locker was…except instead of the row of ugly brown lockers…there was plastic wrap taped all over them, sawhorses sitting about, saw dust on the floor, and power saws on tables ready to go. In front of it all was a large "Construction Zone" sign, with "Keep Out!" written in big letters.

"What the fuck!?!" Clayton said to himself as he took in the scene.

"Guess nobody told you, eh?" a voice came, and Clayton spun around. There standing at the corner he'd just turned was Carl, the head janitor, er…custodian…at Hillsdale High School. Seeing his perplexed look, Carl continued. "School Board finally decided to build that new weight room the football team's been clamoring over for years. Hired the fanciest construction company in town, Hayes Builds, and they just started this week." He shrugged. "As you can see, this whole section of lockers has been shut down."

"So where am I supposed to put my stuff?" Clayton said, exasperation in his voice.

Carl nodded as he turned around, motioning for Clayton to follow him. "Usually that'd be a problem, what with all the new students transferring in from other areas. In fact, talk just a few days ago was that you'd be locker-less for most of the year."

"Locker-less!" Clayton nearly shouted. The idea of not having a locker and lugging six heavy textbooks around by backpack all day…well, it certainly didn't appeal to him.

Carl gave a snicker at Clayton's distress. "Don't worry. The Board decided to open up a stretch of hallway that hasn't been opened in years, and *that's* where you'll find your new locker."

New locker…abandoned…? The thoughts rushed through Clayton's mind as the two rushed through the now-empty hallways, the sounds of teachers' voices coming through to them from the closed classroom doors. It didn't take long for Clayton to realize what Carl was talking about, though. Another few turns brought them to the hallway by Room 237.

Room 237…oh, the stories that students told about it and the rooms beyond it…the ones they couldn't see. Supposedly it was haunted by the original builder of the school, who'd died in a cave-in while constructing the basement. Or a crazy teacher had killed all her students there one year, on the last day of school before summer vacation. And who could forget the story of the group of satanic teachers that'd used the room to summon a portal to Hell? There were other tales, of course, but *totally* unbelievable. Every year that Clayton had been at Hillsdale, everything beyond Room 237 had been sealed-off…and not just with plastic construction wrapping, but really sealed-off, with thick plywood and a real door, one with a serious lock that took a really big key. But for the first time, instead of seeing that plywood and that door, he saw a typical high school hallway, rows of lockers, and several more doors leading to classrooms that hadn't been used in…

"Haven't used this section in near thirty years," Carl said as they paused for a moment. "Usually, this section of lockers wouldn't be used, but with the construction and all, well…school didn't have much choice. Now all you's around the work zone have been moved here.

Clayton stared out at the now-never-used 300-350 section of lockers. They were as plain as could be; nothing set them apart from the hundreds more in the rest of the school. He noticed that most were without locks, though some had one.

"Which one is mine?" he asked.

"Just pick out anyone you want. We already took your locks and things from your old lockers. Pick one out and I'll have it ready for you before next period."

"Well…" Clayton went, scanning the lockers…and then he noticed it. The Master Lock combination lock with the pink number face instead of the typical black…and just below that face, a little rainbow pride flag sticker. It was Jennifer Hurley's lock!

"I'll take that one there," Clayton said, gesturing to the locker next to hers.

"Number three-thirty-two," Carl said, taking out a notepad from his pocket to write the number down, "cool. You'll be all set by next period, which starts in…" he glanced at his watch and whistled, "…just about thirty minutes." He looked back up at Clayton. "You'd better run."

For the first time since gym class two years ago, Clayton did.

~~~

The second-hand on the clock didn't tick, it spun…and way too slowly for Clayton's taste.

He'd been staring at the damn thing for the past five minutes, silently willing the hand to move faster so he could get out of this damn detention and on his way home. He'd wound up there after showing up to Period One over twenty minutes late. Now here he was with all the dweeb-heads, stoners, wasteoids and other losers. All because of that stupid new locker.

At least Carl had been true to his word and had put all his stuff in and his old lock on. The school had all the combos, so it was no surprise they could just open and close them at will. Now that he had his lock back, though, it gave him a sense of security and privacy. He just had to hit that locker up, grab a few things, and then off to a night of playing games at home.

BBRRINGGG!!!

Finally! Clayton thought as the bell went off, signaling the end of that late period of the day. He and the others flew from the detention hall and to wherever they were going. Clayton headed to his new locker. His mind was on the games he'd play later that night on the computer, so he messed-up on the first try with the combo. He concentrated…but couldn't get it the second time, either.

"C'mon!" he said, trying a third time. Again, it wouldn't open when he reached the last number and tugged on the lock. He tried a fourth time…a fifth…and a sixth.

"Damn it!" he shouted out, anger rising in him…anger at the lock, detention, Colton Hayes, high school, and life in general. He banged his head against the locker.

CHUNK!
~~~

His head still against the locker, he opened his eyes and looked down. The lock was laying on the hallway floor, open. He stepped back, a perplexed look on his face. That's when the door of the locker slowly swung open.

For the briefest of moments, Clayton wasn't looking at his windbreaker jacket hanging there, some books at the bottom, and various papers and other junk on the top shelf. Instead it was a swirling, cloudy abyss. Pink and purple hues were punctuated by flashes of yellow lighting in the distance. He blinked his eyes…and the scene was gone. It was just his locker again, full of all his stuff.

Clayton was standing there in a near-state of shock, so didn't hear the approaching footfalls from down the hall. If he would have, he'd have looked over to see Colton Hayes coming toward him, a diabolical look of mischief in his eyes. The star of the football team didn't really hate Clayton, he just knew that the 'loser' was beneath him and had to be treated accordingly. It was the high school way. So when he saw Clayton standing there he shoved him forward, into the lockers.

"Oof!" Clayton went, his face hitting the locker next to his.

"Watch where you're going, geek!" Colton shouted, already several feet down the hallway.

Clayton frowned as the football player's laughter echoed down the hallway. "I hope you die, you stupid fuck!" he said under his breath, then grabbed his things and closed the locker and headed home.

Behind him, the locker gave off a faint, red glow.

<p style="text-align:center">~~~</p>

When Clayton got to school the next morning, he could tell right away that something was wrong.

Students were milling about in front of the building, worried looks on their faces. Some were even crying. On top of that, a police car was parked nearby in the loading zone, though its lights were off and no officer was present.

Clayton scanned the crowd to see if he knew someone but couldn't see anyone he'd want to ask as to what was happening. And not wanting another tardy, he just headed in and to his locker. On the way he ran into Rory, a once-geeky student like Clayton, but one that'd lately been trying to break out of that role. It'd pretty much only caused him trouble, like more beatings from the jocks and more trips to detention.

"Dude, did you hear?"

"No, what?"

"Colton Hayes is dead!"

That stopped Clayton and he looked over at Rory. "What do you mean…*he's dead?* I just saw him last night, after detention." Well, *saw* wasn't really the right word, Clayton thought to himself as he remembered his head getting slammed into the locker.

Rory folded his arms across his chest. "Died last night, right here at school, in the weight room."

"*What?!?*"

Rory nodded. "Was doing a late-night lifting session when a cable broke and the weight he was pumping came down and pumped *him*. From what I hear…fucker got his whole chest caved in. Spit blood up *everywhere*."

"Bull*shit!*" Clayton said, but Rory just shrugged.

"Whatever, man," he said as he started to walk off. "You'll be hearing about it all day. Word's that the principle *himself* is gonna make some big announcement first period."

Clayton watched him go, an uncertain look on his face.

Sure enough, one of the first things in First Period was the announcement of Colton's tragic death the night before, and how police and grief counselors were on hand if anyone needed them. From the gasps he heard in class – mostly from the preppy types, jocks and popular girls – he figured a lot of people would need them. But not him. Clayton didn't really give a fuck. He was happy, in fact, though wouldn't admit it to anyone and even felt bad about it. But the truth was, Colton was a major asshole, and his life would be better without his bullying.

<div align="center">~~~</div>

The rest of the day passed in the usual blur, though interrupted by the grief so many were expressing over the football player. Clayton encountered this firsthand before Fifth Period when Jennifer finally showed up at her locker. When she saw Clayton there and noticed him look over at her, she almost burst into tears.

"Oh, God – isn't it awful!" she sobbed.

"Uh…yeah, I mean, yeah," Clayton said, not sure what to say or do as she looked at him. Clayton couldn't help but notice how hot she was, *still* was. She'd gained a bit of weight over the summer – some said too much, including the cheerleading team, which had her booted from starting squad just a week before classes started. She wasn't *kicked off*, but was too self-conscious to try out again. And since then, she'd only put on more pounds. But to Clayton, she looked even more beautiful, more curvaceous. He thought about her many times at night, and now she was *actually talking* to *him*.

But she just sobbed, and for good reason. For the past two years, she and Colton had been an item. They were the most popular couple in school – the head of the football team and the head of the cheerleading squad. But cracks were beginning to show in their relationship. Jennifer had started to put on weight; Colton's eye had begun to wander. It wasn't long before Colton was spending more time with Felicity, the second-best cheerleader. Of course that rubbed Jennifer the wrong way, and many thought the two could be heading for a breakup. That was the big news as the school year had started. But now Colton was dead…Jennifer was crying…and Clayton seemed to be caught in the middle.

She looked up at him with a sniffle after he said his words. "Th…Th…Thanks," she managed, wiping her tears on the back of her hand.

"Uh…yeah," Clayton said, embarrassed and not sure what to say or do as one of the hottest girls in school stared up at him. God, he wanted to take her right then and there, right in the hallway. Instead he did what he thought was best. "I…I…I gotta get to class!" he said, then spun on his heel and quickly hurried down the hall, away from Jennifer.

<div align="center">~~~</div>

Jennifer watched Clayton speed away before turning back to her own locker. Her mind was lost in grief and she couldn't concentrate on school. She made a decision to head to the office to see the nurse, hoping she could be sent home early. She just had to wait for all this traffic in the hallway to die-down first.

It seemed that all the cool kids were now using the newly-opened hallway as a quicker exit to the parking lot and the expensive, daddy-bought cars that awaited them there. That's why Felicity Chambers was walking down the hallway at the same time that Jennifer was putting the last of her newly acquired Squad B cheer training outfit away. Felicity saw this and couldn't help but snicker to her friend, pointing all the while.

"See, Brianna…this is where you end up if you can't make the team." Beside her, Brianna did her best to hide her smile as Jennifer looked up.

Jennifer frowned. Felicity was still mega-hot and still had that great figure. Brianna was a little taller and had a few more curves, but she was still drop-dead gorgeous. Just a year ago, Jennifer would have been right there will 'em, no one holding a candle to their beauty. But the final throes of puberty weren't kind to Jennifer. She'd put on more pounds than she'd care to admit over the summer and no matter how hard she worked, she couldn't seem to get back to her previous weight. It was killing her confidence, making her feel not so popular, not so special. So Felicity's comment hurt even more, as it was intended. Both young women knew that the main Squad A was where it was at, and with Jennifer now gone from the troop she once dominated, so too was her reputation around the school.

Jennifer Hayes' popularity was on the line, she and everyone knew it.

"Have fun at *second* practice tomorrow," Felicity said over her shoulder as she and Brianne made it to the doors to the parking lot. They laughed loud and happily as they went into the afternoon sun.

"God, I hate her!" Jennifer said under her breath as she started to close her locker and put the lock back on. Here she was, in the throes of grief, and Felicity didn't even care. "I wish *she'd* put on some weight and lose *her* spot on the team. Then we'll see how *she* feels!"

Jennifer slammed her locker shut and stormed from the hallway, going for the same door that Felicity had just exited.

Hopefully tomorrow will be better, she thought as she left the building. Behind her, Locker 332 took on a red glow for just a moment, as if happy.

~~~

It was early morning and both squads of the cheer team were in the school gym, going through their practice moves. The head of the
~~~

football team might be dead, but there was still a game on Friday. And that meant girls to cheer them on, which required practice.

The girls would strut and dance and shake their stuff, while every so often they'd come together and the couple boys on the team would lift them up and toss them into the air, falling safely back into their arms a moment later.

The squads were in the midst of that practice when Felicity came through the door, a good twenty minutes late. The sight of her stopped everyone in their tracks, and caused quite a few mouths to hang open.

"Oh…my…God," many of the others girls said under their breath as they saw Felicity waddle onto the court. Brianne rushed over to her friend.

"Felicity…my God…what's wrong with you?" she said, moving her eyes up and down over Felicity's body.

For her part, Felicity almost broke down in tears. "I don't know!" she nearly sobbed. "I just woke up this morning and I was like…this!"

She held her arms out so Brianne could take in the sight of her. Whereas the night before she'd been a fit and trim five-foot-six and 120 pounds, now she looked much shorter and much fatter. It seemed as if her weight had doubled, and the poor girl almost looked like a balloon.

"God, Felicity," Coach Sommers said, coming over, "did you eat something bad last night that you had an allergic reaction to? You're all puffed up and bloated."

"That must have been it, Coach," Felicity says.

"Well," the coach said, shaking her head in frustration, "get over to your spot and start your warm-ups. We have a big meet this Friday!"

"Um…" Felicity started to say, her face turning a bit red with embarrassment, "I'm not sure I can do that today."

Coach just rolled her eyes. "Fine, take a seat on the bench, then."

As everyone watched, Felicity began walking across the gym to the stands to sit this practice out. But as she moved, it was almost like she was getting…bigger. Her legs seemed to grow larger, bulging out her sweatpants. Her arms grew, to an almost cartoonish size. And her chest and stomach and butt all jutted out more than they had just a minute before.

These changes weren't going unnoticed with Felicity, either. She was totally conscious of the other girls' eyes on her, and did her best to increase her speed. It was hard. She wasn't used to moving so much weight around. And then it happened.

SNAP!

"AAwww!" Felicity screamed as a bone in her leg snapped, no longer able to carry all the weight. A second later the other leg did the same.

Felicity crashed to the gym floor in a heap and lay there, crying out in pain…even as her body continued to grow in size. At first the other students started to rush over to her…but as they saw her body growing and changing, they stopped and then started to back away.

"My God…what's happening!" Brianne cried out, but no one could give an answer, they could just watch in shock.

There before them, Felicity continued to grow and grow. She cried and squealed and begged for someone to stop it, but all anyone could do was stare. The fat seemed to come from nowhere, just growing out of her. It was clear it was heavy and weighing her down. It was growing out from her neck, nearly smothering her whole head.

CRUNCH!

Then it came, the awful sound of the heavy fat crushing the remaining bones in Felicity's body as well as her internal organs. Blood flew from every available orifice, covering the gym floor.

The students screamed and ran, trying their best to get away from the grizzly sight of Felicity's dead and deformed body.

~~~

By the time Clayton got to school an hour or so later, news of Felicity's death had spread and everyone was talking about it. It wasn't just hushed whispers, either, but open talk about the gruesome way she'd died…and how she'd looked beforehand.

Clayton wasn't really sure what was happening. It wasn't every week that you had two of the most popular people in school bite the dust like that. He sighed. *There's nothing I can do about it.* With that thought, he headed through the busy hallway and toward his new locker. The day took on a new and better feel when he reached it…for he saw that Jennifer was there at her locker, too.

She had to be feeling awful, so Clayton made a point to choose his
~~~

words carefully. He got to his locker, opened it up, and only then did he look over at Jennifer, who was doing her best not to cry. He noticed this and offered a comforting word.

"I'm real sorry about your teammate. I didn't know her but–"

Clayton's words were interrupted as Jennifer lunged toward him, wrapping him in a hug.

"Oh, isn't it awful!" she sobbed, letting the tears come unbidden.

"I'm…I'm sorry," Clayton said, perplexed and surprised. After a moment he put his arms around her, patting her on the back a few times. He didn't think he'd ever gotten a hug from a girl his age, not like that before.

"It's all my fault!" Jennifer said, though her words were hard to make out over her sobbing.

Clayton narrowed his eyes to that, confused. "How could it be your fault? From what I heard, she ate something bad and…and…"

He trailed-off, not sure what else to say. *How could you eat something that'd make you gain a hundred pounds overnight?* It just didn't make any sense, but then, neither did what Jennifer was saying to him.

"No," she said, a bit more control in her voice as she pulled away and looked into his eyes, "I mean, I caused this."

"How?"

"I wished she'd die…right here, yesterday just as school was getting out." She sobbed again. "I said it out loud!"

Clayton rolled his eyes and smiled. "That's silly. You can't just *wish* for someone to die and then…"

He let the words die in his mouth, realizing what he was saying. For that's exactly what he'd done with Colton…mentioning that he'd wish he'd just die…and he did. Now Jennifer was telling him she'd done much the same with Felicity, and now *she* was dead.

A far-off, perplexed look came across Clayton's face as he puzzled out what exactly was going on. He didn't get too far before some shouting broke his train of thought.

Behind them, an argument was breaking out and it drew their attention. It was between Rory and Mr. Pingle, the biology teacher.

"Fuck you and your damn detention!" Rory shouted.

"You'll be there or you'll get another from me tomorrow," Mr. Pingle yelled after him.

"Drop dead, asshole!" Rory shouted back before he dashed out the doors to the parking lot. Behind him, Mr. Pingle made to follow, thought better of it, shook his head and muttered "damn kids" under his breath, and started back to his classroom.

Clayton looked over at Jennifer to see her reaction. That's when he saw a faint red glow emanating from his locker, though it faded away just as he looked.

"Did you see that?" he said, putting his hand on Jennifer's back to turn her toward the locker, but a ghastly sound from Mr. Pingle's room stopped him.

"No…no…NO!!! Aaahhh!!!"

CRASH!

Clayton and Jennifer looked at one another, then both bolted toward the classroom that the scream and crash had come from. They reached the door just as half a dozen other students did the same. There in the biology lab was Mr. Pingle, lying on the floor, his body totally visible except for his head…which was crushed under a large and heavy bookcase that had been set up against the wall. Blood was already starting to flow from under the bookcase to a drain in the middle of the floor.

Beside him, Jennifer screamed and another student started to throw-up.

Eyes wide, Clayton turned from the scene. He was in shock, not from seeing Mr. Pingle lying there dead, but from what he thought was really happening. As other students rushed to the doorway of the biology lab to peer in, Clayton stepped away, his mind working.

I wished Colton would die…and he did, he puzzled out in his mind. *Then Jennifer wished Felicity would die…and* she *did*. He looked at the locker, remembering that faint red glow of a moment ago. *And then Rory said out loud for Mr. Pingle to die…and* he *did*.

The wheels in Clayton's head stopped turning as the truth of the matter clicked into place.

"The locker's killing 'em!" he said to himself in a whisper, then repeated it louder. "The locker's killing 'em! It has to be!"

He spun around, looking for Jennifer. But the hallway was already filling up, a lot more than usual. People from all over the school were rushing to that spot to see what'd happened, to see the gruesome scene for themselves. All the while, they talked in hushed tones over one another.

"He's dead."

"…was killed by something…"

"It just fell on him!"
"He was killed…"
"He died…"
"Kill…die…kill…"
"Clayton…!"
"…Kill…
"Clayton!"

The shout cut through the cacophony of voices, allowing Clayton to focus. He saw Jennifer up ahead, waving at him like she had something urgent to say. *Maybe she's figured it out, too!* Clayton thought to himself as he started toward her, wending his way through the throng of students. He didn't notice the faint glow of his locker.

"Jennifer!" he yelled, trying to be heard over the din. He began moving toward her, an inch-by-inch slog through the packed body of students. Then it happened.

CRACK…CRUNCH…CRASH!

Clayton heard the noise and looked up just in time to see one of the overhead fluorescent light displays crack open. His eyes widened as one of the long lightbulbs jaggedly broke off from its base and started to fall…right at him!

He didn't have a chance to yell and couldn't get his hands up in time, either. The long bulb fell down toward him, managed to flip in midair, and the jagged end that'd broken off slammed into his face.

Blood flew everywhere as the bulb embedded itself in Clayton's eye. The force of it pushed him back and down. He fell to the floor, his good eye staring sightlessly up at the ceiling as life fled him.

Jennifer saw it all and screamed, a cry that was taken up by many others in the hallway. They ran from the scene, yelling and shouting what'd happened. Words like "die" and "kill" were intermixed with the names of friends and teachers and even parents as students panicked and ran.

Behind them, Locker 332 glowed red.

THE END

13. CAMPSITE #9

It was the week before classes started up again and Jim had finally gotten everyone together for a camping trip.

They were going to Holland Lake, a gorgeous spot just up in the Swan Mountain range. Jim had been there numerous times growing up and he wanted to show some of the out-of-staters what it was like. He *especially* wanted to show Wendy.

He'd had the hots for her ever since PSYCH 311 during fall semester last year. It'd taken until PSYCH 352 the next spring for him to work up the nerve to talk to her. Now, with his final fall semester approaching, he wasn't going to let her get away. Holland Lake was just the place for that to happen.

There were five of them heading up: Jim and Wendy, plus Jim's best friend Ray and his girlfriend, Cynthia. Tagging along was Cynthia's younger sister, Debra, who was still in high school.

They drove in Ray's beat up old van, taking the scenic, winding two-lane highway up from the university town of Missoula, past the touristy Seeley Lake, and then down a long dirt road to the campground.

The lake wasn't that large, just 400 acres in area, and was dominated by Holland Peak, a towering sedimentary stone monolith that had been carved out by glaciers 170 million years before. It was every bit as visually stunning as the peaks in Glacier National Park, a little more than a hundred miles to the north of them, but with a fraction of the people.

"Damn, looks full," Ray said as he pulled into the campground.

"This is just the day-use area," Jim replied. "Head into the loop over there where the camping spots are. We'll find something."

Jim was certain they'd be alright. It was the middle of the week, after all, and not the busier weekend times.

"Ray's right," Cynthia chimed-in. "I'm not seeing an open spot anywhere."

Jim took a moment to take his eyes from Wendy's legs and looked out the window. Sure enough, it was plate after plate from California or Washington or some other neighboring state, nearly all with a huge RV and a generator going.

"We might have to go back," Debra chimed-in from the back. It was no secret she didn't really want to be on this trip, was more satisfied with air-conditioning and her iPhone.

"Shut up, Deb," Cynthia said. "I'm *not* driving all the way back to Missoula."

"Maybe that's not a bad idea," Wendy said, getting sick of Jim's wandering eyes.

Jim frowned. Things were falling apart fast "Well…there *is* one spot…" he started to say.

"Uh, duh…where is it?" came Ray's frustrated reply.

"It's off the beaten path…not really used anymore, and, well…"

"Well, what?" Cynthia said.

"Well…"

Jim thought of all the stories he'd heard over the years, about the girl that'd gone missing, how her ghost was still about, mad as hell and eager to make anyone else suffer the same fate. But those were just stories…weren't they?

"*Well?*" Ray said, tension growing in his voice. "I'm sick of driving around this loop and the people behind me are startin' to get pissed."

"Well…it's just overgrown a bit," Jim said, an uneasy smile on his face.

"Overgrown?" Cynthia laughs. "Why, that's no problem at all."

"Hell no," Ray agrees. "Now where is it?"

Jim points the way, and soon the van is weaving through some low-hanging branches and brushing up against bushes. It's clear the small road they're on hasn't been cleared for vehicles in some time, years most likely.

And then they were there, passing a marker that said #9.

There was nothing particularly out of the ordinary about the #9 campsite. In fact, it was about as typical as you could get.

A simple gravel driveway off the main, paved thoroughfare through the campground. A few feet off, two picnic tables pushed together to create one long table, painted dark, Forest Service green. Nearby was the firepit, a metal-enclosed circle with an attached grill that could be folded down to set over the fire. A few large trees circled the site, one with a thick nail driven into it, likely a hook to hang food to keep it out of reach of bears. The whole site was no more than thirty-feet-square…but what made it a little different from the other eight campsites in the loop was its location on the edge.

The whole Holland Lake campground jutted up against the Swan Mountain range, and in this particular spot it was right below Holland peak. It was some kind of geologic upthrust that'd happened millions of years ago – Jim couldn't remember the exact story in the guidebook, and he wasn't that interested in looking it up – and they soared very high above.

It gave the campsite a kind of imposing look, making you feel overshadowed by the large mountain right next to you. The air was dry and, strangely, there weren't that many sounds from birds or other animal life. The rest of the campsite loop *was* noisy, but not this area.

"C'mon, it's the best one in the loop," Jim said.

The others had to admit *that* much, and that was mostly because of the privacy that this area of the campground afforded. Being off and away as this area was, you weren't right next to the other campers.

The rest of the day went well. After getting the van unloaded they set up their tents, inflated their floatable rafts, and spent the next few hours on the water. As dusk grew closer they got the fire going, cooked their hotdogs, and cracked open their first beers. By the time full darkness came, all five were settled around the flames, laughing and joking and telling stories. Most had to do with school, summer jobs, and of course the area they were camping at.

"I mean, just *look* at this place," Ray said, "it's perfect for a scary movie." The others laughed, though Jim not so much. Ray didn't notice and continued on. "I'm tellin' ya…it's right out of a fuckin' Eighties teen horror flick, the real shitty kind. First we got the strange locale," he continues, raising his arms up to take in the surroundings, "then we got us the horny college-age kids." The others laugh a bit to that.

"But aren't we missing a few?" Cynthia laughs. "After all, where's the concerned forest ranger, and – last but not least – the strange and crazy mountain man loner that shows up to warn us."

Everyone laughs and drinks more of their beers.

Wendy wasn't quite feeling it as much as the others, though. In fact, she was feeling quite a bit groggy, mostly from hiking around the lake and all that swimming, not to mention the lack of food, she told herself, and not the beer. But it was certainly the beer that was making her see…*what, exactly?*

It was like a flash of white in the trees, just at the firelight's edge. She narrowed her eyes, trying to get a better idea of what it was.

Probably just my imagination, she thought…but then saw it again. A white flash, but more this time – a flash of movement, like a person.

"Guys…" she started, bringing her arm up and pointing off in that direction of the woods, "…did you see that?"

It took a few moments for people to quiet down and stop their laughing and joking enough to notice her.

"What is it?" Jim finally said, getting up from his spot at the fire and walking over to her. He knelt down and peered into the woods where she was pointing.

"I thought I saw…*something*," Wendy answers.

"Oo-ooh-oh – ghosts!" Ray says, jumping up and doing a little dance, spilling beer on himself all the while. This elicited quite a few more laughs, and Jim couldn't help but snicker beside Wendy. Suddenly, she felt quite silly.

"It was probably nothing," she says, feeling her face growing red.

"Yeah, probably nothing," Jim repeats beside her before getting up and going back to his spot.

"I'm just gonna…" Wendy says getting up, but she trails-off. She doesn't really need to go to the bathroom…she just wanted a few moments to herself. She also wanted to check and see if there was something there…mostly to prove she wasn't losing her own mind.

"Don't get lost," Ray said chidingly as she started to head into the darkness of the trees.

"Here," Cynthia said, getting up and rushing to her. She handed her a roll of toilet paper and grasped her arm. "Just keep the firelight in sight – you'll be fine."

Wendy gave a forced smile as Cynthia rushed back to Ray's side, and then she turned and headed into the dark. She only went a couple dozen feet, keeping the fire in sight all the while. She did her business and started to get up. That's when she saw it again…that flash of white movement.

"Hello…is anyone there?"

No answer came to her call. She glanced over her shoulder. The campfire was now a distant light, at least thirty feet away. She felt scared to be this far, and yet some overwhelming compulsion had her moving further away from that comforting light, closer to whatever was in the darkness. She just *had* to know…even though she didn't know why.

She took a few more steps, then the movement, the white flash. This time she saw it clearly for what it was – a white dress. It was covering a young girl. Wendy couldn't see her face due to the long black hair. Fear gripped hold of her, but again, she just couldn't help taking a few steps forward.

Then it came. The white right was in front of her. It made such a contrast to the dark black hair. It was a girl, probably no older than ten.

"Are you…" Wendy started, making to ask if the girl was okay. Instead the girl looked up at her quickly. The black hair fell away, and Wendy's eyes went wide. She tried to scream but couldn't.

Back at the campfire, the others started to grow concerned when Wendy didn't come back.

"It's been over five minutes now," Jim said, but Ray just shook his head.

"Too many hotdogs. Let Mother Nature run her course."

But not everyone felt the same. "She's been too long," Cynthia said as she got up. "I'll go and take a look," adding, "I'm sure she's fine."

"I'll go too," Deb said, rushing up to join her, and her older sister nodded.

"Aw shit, guess that means I better–"

"No," Cynthia said, cutting-off Ray's words, "we'll be fine."

That was fine with Ray, who settled back down with his beer. Jim looked like he was going to argue for a moment, but a look at Cynthia told him that wouldn't be a good idea. So the two let the two women go, confident they'd find Wendy and all three would be back shortly.

The two walked to where they thought Wendy would have gone. Cynthia pulled out a flashlight she'd grabbed and waved it about.

"There," Deb said, pointing off into the darkness to their side, "did you see that?"

"See what?"

"That flash of white…like something was moving."

Cynthia shook her head in the dark, even though Deb couldn't see it. "Wendy was wearing yellow."

"Let's just check it out," Deb says with a sigh.

The two start over that way, and while doing so, Cynthia sees the flash of white.

"See it?" Deb says.

"Yeah, I saw it."

"What is it?"

Cynthia shrugged. *Beats me*, she thought…but at the same time, she had to find out.

The two continued on, waving the flashlight before them. Then they saw it…or more rightly, *her*.

"Oh…my…God…" Deb said, her eyes falling on Wendy. The young woman's usual healthy glow and youthful look was gone. Instead her blonde hair had turned a whitish-gray, the skin on her face had shriveled up like she was a hundred years old, and her mouth was open in a permanent silent scream.

Then both women saw a flash of light out of the corner of their eye. Cynthia shot the flashlight that way, illuminating a young girl in white, black hair covering her face. Both women looked on as the girl slowly raised her head, the hair falling away to reveal that face.

Both screamed, a blood-curdling sound that reverberated through the mountains around them.

~~~

No one really knows what happened to the five campers that went up to Holland Lake that summer.

Authorities pieced together what they thought had happened…but it made no sense.

They'd found Wendy's body right away, though what on earth could have happened to it, they had no clue. Nothing they'd ever heard of, no creature of the woods, could ever have caused *that*.

No sign of the other four were ever found. It was figured the five went camping, something happened to Wendy, and the other four went to investigate. Nearly everyone in the campground that night testified to hearing that awful scream around midnight.

The Forest Service rangers figured Wendy had gone out to do her business, saw something, screamed, and the others came running to help. But whatever she'd seen not only got her but had gotten them, too. Finally, the government chalked the whole incident up to…bears. File shut, case closed.

Old-timers knew that was a load of hooey. No, the ghost of Holland Lake had struck again.

THE END
~~~

14. INDIAN BURIAL GROUND

I know a secret Indian burial ground that no one else does.

I stumbled upon its location while doing some research work in the archives of the local historical society. Even the local Indians don't even know of it anymore…the few that still call the town of Paradise home.

Seems the place was in wide use up until the late-1880s. Then most of the Cree Indian tribes in the area were shunted-off to the reservation. The last body was put in the ground there in 1887 and then the cemetery sat for years. There were no grave markers like the Christian cemeteries had, no real way to discern where the bodies were buried. And once the Indians were gone, the whites tended to forget.

By 1911, the whole burial ground area had been plowed over and left as fields for grazing cattle. It stayed that way for a few years before turning into a training area for the boys that'd volunteered to fight the Germans in Europe. When that was all done a few years later it went back to empty fields. Then someone decided to plant corn on it. So it grew corn for over twenty years. After another fight with the Germans the country was growing so much that new land was needed to build houses. The old corn fields that'd been there 'forever' were chosen as the initial parcels of a large subdivision that'd eventually hold over one hundred homes. The first shovels went into the ground in 1948 and the first house was completed the next year. The Harris family moved in just before Christmas 1949.

By all accounts, the family was happy. A husband and wife and two young kids. The newspaper accounts of the time couldn't figure out why he'd snapped. Stress from his insurance job was the only explanation, even though his boss said he'd always been happy. It took quite some time for the neighborhood to get over the news. After all, it wasn't everyday a man just took an axe and killed his whole family and then himself.

It was a huge shock to the neighborhood and the talk of the area for months. The stain of the incident hung over the house for some time. But life went on, and over time people forgot. Eventually a new family moved in. They were happy.

That happiness turned to misery two months later. No one could figure out why the twin girls had missed two days of school in a row, or why their mother hadn't been reachable on the phone. When they visited the house they found the door open and the bodies of the girls and their mother inside, throats cut. The husband was in the garage, hanging from a garden hose, the bloody knife lying at his feet on the floor.

The house was bulldozed to the ground after that. The homeowner's association decided not to rebuild. Instead, that parcel would become a park. So the dump trucks and backhoes were brought in one day, and the next there were slides and jungle gyms and swings and see-saws. Children from all over the neighborhood came to play. Life was good, people were happy.

Their happiness was shattered one summer afternoon when all the chains on the swings broke simultaneously, sending four children flying swiftly through the air. They landed hard on the jungle gym, where they fell to the ground after hitting every bar on the way down. Three of the poor youngsters died.

People started talking after that; the old stories were remembered.

"Bad karma left over from the war camps…"

"All that bad juju from the fighting…"

"Maybe it had something to do with those Indians…"

It was those old-timer memories that got the ball rolling. Talk started up about the Cree tribe that'd lived in the area over a hundred years before. Some remembered their grandparents talking about the spots they lived at, what areas they inhabited before the town grew up around them and forced them to move on.

That's when quite a few of the town's prominent citizens came to the local newspaper to make some inquiries. I was working the night desk when they barged-in, demanding to see the archives.

"Come on back first thing when we open," I finally said to assuage them, and it worked. They shuffled out, satisfied the truth could wait until morning…especially with their favorite new episodes on the TV that night.

But I didn't wait until the morning. Instead I headed back into the archives myself, did a few quick searches, and discovered the Indian burial ground.

The subdivision where all the problems had been occurring was built right over it, and it seemed the ceremonial center of the grounds was situated right where the current park was built.

No wonder they're having so many problems, I thought to myself as I deleted those entries from the computer, tore up their physical counterparts from the old newspapers.

Then I got ready for the long drive home, to Stillwater, a town located over fifty miles from Paradise.

That's where most of the Cree Indians like myself lived…ever since we'd been kicked from our homeland over a hundred years before.

THE END

15. THE GIRL NEXT DOOR

Kyle couldn't believe this was happening; he couldn't believe *she* was actually talking to *him*! But more than that…she actually seemed to *want* him. Yes, for the first time ever, Kyle Flind was going to get laid…and by the girl of his dreams.

My God, Kyle thought, *this is the best day of my life!*

~~~

It'd all started earlier that summer when someone *finally* moved into the forest green house at the end of the block. It was two stories with a basement and a garage and a pretty nice yard, too. Yeah…pretty much the same as all the other houses on that part of Hickory Street. Nothing really to set it apart…aside from who moved
~~~

in.

Her name was Stephanie, and she looked to be about 17 or 18…maybe even 19 or 20. Kyle always had a hard time telling how old girls were once they reached…that point.

He was just 17, himself. Just turned it a month before, and only a few weeks after school got out for the summer. Just one year left at the ol' Stillwater High School, and then off to the local community college. Electrician was the route he and his dad had decided on. It would keep him off the road, unlike the old man, who was on sales calls five to six days a week.

That was the case when Stephanie had moved in just a week after school let out. Dad had been off on business and Kyle was repainting the front fence. He'd had a good view of the moving van – California plates, the usual this far north – as well as the beauty that its contents belonged to. Neither he nor the moving men had been able to keep their eyes off her.

She had long blonde hair, done up in some kind of retro fashion, like one of those TV shows about the 60s. She wore dark sunglasses and bright red lipstick. A tank top and a miniskirt showed off her amazing shoulders and stunning legs. And those tits…my God, those tits!

Kyle was in love the moment he'd laid eyes on her, and judging from how most of the men in the neighborhood were acting, they were, too. Husbands suddenly found the time to mow the lawn or fix the front light…things that had been postponed for a football game or fishing with the guys for who-knows-how-long. Wives quickly appeared, scolding and demanding that something be taken care of in the house, *anything* to get them back inside and out of sight of…of…*her.*

He still remembered the first time she'd talked to him.

"Hi, what's your name?"

The question had startled Kyle from his reverie…which he hadn't known he'd been in until she'd spoken and he'd looked up.

"Um…uh…I…um…" he managed, staring up from where he was crouched down by the fence and the paint bucket. There before him was…*her*…the girl moving in. But how'd she sneak up on him so fast. He'd only taken his eyes off her for a moment and…

She cocked her head to one side and gave a slight smile. One hand moved up to her face and she tilted the sunglasses down from her eyes to perch precariously on her nose. Then she stared at him and that smile grew larger. If Kyle thought he was at a loss for words earlier…now he didn't think he even had a mouth left to speak with!

"My name's Stephanie…Stephanie Miller," she said, and with one quick motion, pushed the sunglasses back over her eyes and then extended her hand to him.

"Um…uh…Kyle…I'm Kyle, and…um…uh…just Kyle…"

His face was so red and so hot he knew he could cook an egg on it in seconds, probably burning it in the process. Her smile only grew bigger, but not in any kind of condescending or off-putting kind of way. It was almost as if…*she liked him.*

"Nice to meet you…Just Kyle," she said with a giggle, then turned on her heel and made to walk away. "Don't be a stranger, neighbor."

And with that she was gone, back inside to unpack, though she did reappear from time to time to walk about the yard…and greet others on the block. She was polite to the wives she encountered, but seemed to be a little more flirty with their husbands…especially those under forty. But it was the younger teens and twenty-something singles that she seemed to pay the most attention to.

After that the moving van left and things quieted down. The usual routine of the neighborhood started up again…nine-to-five workweeks, date-night-Friday's, outing-Saturday's, and barbeque-Sundays. It was the typical suburbia affair and looked to be the start of another typical summer.

Then Mr. Fagen down the street went missing. Kyle had first noticed when the police car showed up and Mrs. Fagen was showing them around, pointing things out. She'd looked frustrated as they'd left. Kyle hadn't seen them again…or Mr. Fagen. Shortly after that, the first 'missing person' sign went up around the neighborhood. It wouldn't be the last.

A week or so after that happened, the young social media professional that always kept to himself disappeared. His mom had driven up from Colorado to figure out why he'd stopped calling and emailing. She had the police with her and a key. They went inside, poked around a bit, and then talked in the yard for a while. The mom looked about as frustrated as Mrs. Fagen had when they'd left her.

Kyle didn't think much of it, and neither did his dad when they spoke of it one night when he was home. It was no secret that the

Fagen's had been having marital problems for years – "Chuck's probably gone down to visit his brother in Key West again" – and everyone knew how flighty and unpredictable the younger social media generation was – "probably on that damn Fentanyl shit."

Kyle's dad seemed to have the answer to everything, so Kyle stopped thinking about it. Until Mat went missing.

Mat Baines was the same age as Kyle, though more popular so they didn't really talk. But they'd been living on Hickory Street together forever, and it just wasn't like Mat to up and leave without telling anyone. No…something wasn't right.

It was about a week after the social media guy went missing that Matt disappeared as well. His parents were frantic, and this time the whole neighborhood was involved. Flyers were posted, search parties were organized, the local news did a big story. But nothing turned up. That last he'd been seen was at home.

"He just said he was going to go out into the yard to practice his throwing," his mom told the TV news. It was no secret that Matt had a good chance of getting to the big leagues one day if he kept up that pitching arm.

Kyle put in three hours on the search, all over town and the surrounding area. Everyone had. Well…everyone but their recent move-in, Stephanie. And that's when Kyle first realized that Matt and Stephanie's houses were right next to each other.

That's how he found himself standing in front of her yard one night around dusk, wondering about Matt. His mind must have wandered, for he didn't hear her approach.

"Howdy, Just Kyle."

"Oh…uh…" Kyle managed, spinning around to see her there.

She was as stunning as ever, in a wispy white summer dress that clung to her in all the right places. Kyle felt a stirring in his pants at the sight of her, and shifted uncomfortably, hoping she wouldn't notice. But she did, looking down, then putting a hand over her mouth as she giggled. Kyle could feel his face getting hot. He looked down at his feet. When he looked up, Stephanie was still staring at him…but this time her look had changed. She seemed more serious, though still quite playful. She bit her lip and toyed with her hair, then let one band of her top slip from her shoulder.

"Uh…" Kyle said, trying to find some words, *any* words.

Stephanie gave a playful turn, flipping her hair over her shoulder. Then she looked back at him…and blew him a kiss before motioning with her finger to follow.

"C'mon," she said, looking over her shoulder at him with that playful grin, "I know you want this." And then she said something that Kyle would never forget. Stopping, she turned back and Kyle was suddenly right up next to her. She looked up into his eyes. "I've wanted this since the first moment I saw you."

Kyle's heart skipped a beat. No girl had ever said that to him. Before he could find words to say, Stephanie lunged up and suddenly their lips were locked in a kiss. It went on for an eternity, to Kyle's reckoning, and when it was done he was slow to open his eyes. When he did so, he saw Stephanie backing away, a smile coming to her face.

"You're such a good kisser!"

"Well…uh…I…"

Stephanie gave another of those playful laughs, then grasped hold of Kyle's hand and began pulling him further into the house. Feeling higher on life than he had in some time, Kyle allowed himself to be pulled in.

The house was pretty standard, though very sparsely furnished. Stephanie had been there for a little over a month so far, but judging by the amount she had unpacked it looked more like a few days. It's not that there were lots of boxes that still needed to be sorted out – there were none in sight – it was just that with the amount of items in the house…well, how could anyone live like this? A single couch, one table and chair, and on the quick glance he saw of the kitchen, just a couple plates and bowls.

"I'm still waiting for most of my stuff to be packed up and shipped to me," Stephanie said as she continued to pull his hand, and as if reading his thoughts. They'd moved from the basic entryway through the living room and were now moving down a hallway toward what must be the main bedroom. Kyle took it all in in a kind of haze, not really believing this was happening, not wanting it to end.

They reached the bedroom door, whereupon Stephanie stopped, turned around to look at him with that smile, and said, "Are you ready for this?"

With a gulp and his best 'I'm ready' smile, Kyle nodded that he was.

"Good," she replied, and then still standing next to him, swung the door open and flipped on the light.

Kyle's eyes went wide and his heart nearly stopped. There in the bedroom was…nothing. Not a bed or dresser or any furniture whatsoever. No clothes or pictures or plants, just very thick, black curtains on the windows. What *was* there was nearly enough to make him gag and throw up. First he noticed Mat, his head hung low as if he was passed out…or maybe even dead. He was halfway up one wall…stuck there with some kind of…cocoon. It's all Kyle could think – like one of those caterpillar cocoons that they use to turn into a butterfly. But Mat was no butterfly. He was surrounded by this thick, slimy mucous-like material, a sickly green-yellow color. It was holding him up on the wall, pinning his arms in place at his sides. Kyle couldn't see the lower half of his body whatsoever, for it was all covered up. And Matt wasn't the only one. There were four more men stuck to the walls as well, each covered with the same strange material. Kyle recognized Mr. Fagen from down the street, as well as the social media guy, but the other two he had no idea. And beneath all of them, nearly covering the entire floor, were all kinds of…eggs. That's all Kyle could think of them ass, large tannish-colored eggs.

"Aren't they beautiful," Stephanie said then, breaking Kyle from the shock of what he was seeing. He glanced over at her, and she was staring with love in her eyes at the eggs on the floor. "My babies," he heard her say faintly under her breath.

Then she slowly turned her gaze up at him, and Kyle's blood nearly froze. There was something different about her, something more menacing. As if sensing this, Stephanie straightened up…and seemed to grow taller in front of him. With wide eyes, Kyle watched as she did in fact grow in size, both height and width, and then she started to slip out of her white dress. She did it quickly and let it drop. She was wearing no underwear…because she really didn't have to. It wasn't the lower-half of a human woman that Kyle was looking at…but some kind of monstrous-freak bottom! She had green, scaley skin and where there should have been a big, beautiful, hairy pussy there was just…snakes.

Those snake-like appendages growing from Stephanie's nether regions shot out at that moment at Kyle, wrapped themselves around him, and the 'heads' of them began to bite into him. Kyle felt some kind of fluid pumping into his veins, and his body began to feel heavier. Suddenly, and with horror, he looked down to see some kind of mucous-like substance forming around his lower legs, moving outward to cover him…just like the others in the room were.

"No!" Kyle shouted, frantically beating at the snakes as they covered him, but it was no use. Soon he was covered entirely, including his arms, which were now pinned to him. Still the snakes did not stop. Still working from Stephanie's lower half, they began to lift Kyle up and the next thing he knew he was stuck to the wall, right next to Matt.

That's when the snakes finally let go of him.

"You taste *good*," Stephanie said as the snakes shot back into her, and she covered herself up again with her dress. Then she looked as though she might be sick, her face taking on a pained and bewildered expression. Suddenly she gagged, and – putting a hand up to her mouth – vomited up an…egg. With a smile she looked at it fondly, then put it down on the floor with the others. She looked up again at Kyle as she made to leave the room.

"Our first child together, Kyle." She laughed. "The first of hundreds!"

Kyle felt desperate as she began to close the door, leaving him alone in the dark with the others. Stephanie laughed and laughed as she made her way back down the hall.

My God, Kyle thought, *this is the worst day of my life!*

THE END

16. THE BATHROOM ON THE FOURTH FLOOR

Carroll College has always been haunted.

It's a Catholic school so has lots of priests. There are stories of some killing themselves over the years. But those are just stories. There are no ghosts.

Late-night walkers have seen the ghost of a student jumping out of a window to kill himself. Sometimes it happens around O'Connell Hall, other times around St. Charles Hall or even All Saints Chapel. But there's no documented case of that suicide ever actually *happening*.

Some said the ghostly sightings went back to when the college's cornerstone was first laid. That'd been way back in 1909, with President William Howard Taft doing the honors. A few think a curse was also laid on the school that day. Most just brush that off as nonsense.

No, the only reported death on campus happened long after that. Many thought the real activity began around then. It was the mid- to late-1960s. That's when a student died in the bathroom on the fourth floor of St. Charles Hall.

No one really knows what happened. The official investigation concluded that he simply blacked-out, fell forward, hit his head on the sink, and then fell to the floor. The porcelain sink didn't break, which caused a major hemorrhage in the young man's brain.

He was still alive when another student found him hours later, though unconscious and barely breathing. He was rushed to the hospital but caught pneumonia. He died a couple of weeks later.

That's when the activity on the fourth floor started.

Many students said they'd be brushing their teeth when, suddenly in the mirror, they'd see not their own reflections staring back at them, but that of a young man, a bloody wound on his head. It'd happen for just a second, but long enough to freak the student out, typically sending them shouting down the hallways in their bathrobe or underwear…if even that.

Some reported turning on the faucet, but instead of water coming out, it ran red with blood.

The stories were shrugged-off by campus administrators until they became too widespread, drawing some of the townsfolk. At that point the bathroom was locked-up and sealed-off. It was the early-1970s. Now it was only opened once a year for inspection of the pipes.

That's when it happened.

Russell hated the yearly inspection. He knew the stories about the young man dying as well as anyone. So far he'd been in charge of the inspections for eight years, ever since his boss, Mr. Wilkins, had retired. *He'd* done them for over fourteen years himself, and without incident. But he always told Russell that he got a strange feeling while in there, like someone…or *something*…was watching him.

With a sigh at that thought from long ago, Russell turned the key in the lock and heard the 'click' of it opening. He turned the knob and was there again, in that bathroom, just like this time last year.

The windows – always opaque to let in little light – were still taped over, so he had to flip the light switch near the door. The fluorescent lights flicked on overhead slowly, one set going on at a time the length of the long bathroom.

There was the old white tiling dating back to the 1940s, which covered the floor and the walls. Mirrors were set over white porcelain sinks, no frames about them. Old-fashioned urinals, very low to the floor, were spaced along one wall, while a set of toilet stalls covered the next. Another had a single large bathtub against it while the final wall had a row of showers, just two with curtains.

It was old-fashioned, not updated and modernized like the other bathrooms on campus. That alone gave Russell the chills. He just hated this part of his job but knew he couldn't delegate it off to anyone else, either. "The responsibility comes with the position," Mr. Wilkins had said before he'd handed the keys off to Russell on his last day of work.

Russell rolled his eyes. Just another three more years until his *own* retirement. Then he'd be done with this bathroom for good. But until then…he had a job to do, and do it he would!

The inspection itself was pretty straightforward – check each of the sinks for leakage, the same with the toilets and shower heads. Last would come the bathtub, a cursory look at the drains, and a final glance at the window fittings. The whole process rarely took more than ten minutes…but those were some of the slowest ten minutes of the whole year.

"Might as well get to it," Russell said, setting down his work bag of tools and keys and other odds-and-ends. He started with the shower stalls. He'd reach up and wiggle the piping that led to the shower head. If no drips came out, he'd bend down and check the drain. When that looked fine, it'd be off to the next.

That done, Russell inspected the toilets much the same way. They were all fine, as was the bathtub. That left only the windows and the sinks. A glance told him the windows were just fine, so that left just the sinks.

Russell hated this part. He'd start off by going to each one, bending down to check the pipe beneath, wiggling it a bit and nudging it. Satisfied it was still tight and not dripping, he'd go on to the next. Within two minutes he was done with the whole row. Well…almost. He always skipped *that* sink, saving it for last.

He called it Sink Number 4. It was the fourth sink from the window. Nothing set it apart from the other sinks in the long row, nothing except its history. Russell knew that history, knew the stories that came after, and hated this part of his job, hated this moment of the year more than anything.

Just three more years, he thought, trying to work up his confidence. To give himself a little boost and to show that it didn't bother him, he wadded-up some spit in his mouth and spat right onto the floor at his feet.

And it worked. With a deep breath he moved forward toward the sink and then he was there.

Just the usual inspection, he told himself as he looked at the faucet, gave it a wiggle then tried the two knobs. Both did nothing and there were no leaks. The drain was fine, as was the pipe beneath.

"Whew!" Russell went, letting out a long sigh of relief. He shook his head and gave a slight smile, even chuckled to himself a bit. It was over – he'd made it another year!

Smiling, Russell began to step away from the sink, his thoughts already on that evening and the football game he'd watch down at Fred's with the guys. It was his turn to buy the wings and the first round and so long as that damn Eddie didn't knock over the...

All thoughts flew from Russell's mind as his eyes caught a glance of the mirror above the sink. There his reflection was, staring back at him as was to be expected, but behind it was...another man!

Russell's eyes went wide and he spun about to see who was behind him. He saw right away that it was no one. But he knew what he saw – the young man with the bloody head!

Russell made to spin back around to look in the mirror again. That's when his foot connected with the wad of spit he'd deposited on the floor. He slipped, the entire weight of his body flying up into the air. He stayed propelled there for a moment before gravity took over and he came crashing down.

THUD!

The porcelain sink was the first think Russell's head met, hitting it hard and knocking his body askance. Next it hit the tiled floor, just as hard. Blood began to pool around Russell's head as he lay on the floor dying.

Just three more years...that last thought went cruelly through his head before death took him.

THE END

17. THE HAUNTED BANK VAULT

The bank on 44th and Latimer is haunted.

On the outside, it looks like another old brick building. But on the inside it has…well, let's just say a 'certain, funky kinda feel.' Most everyone in Applewood knew it, too. And the stories…oh, *the stories!* The building itself had plenty. It was old, built in the late-1800s. It'd always been a bank, with the customer service windows on the spacious first floor, which was really the size of two, the way the ceiling stretched so high above.

Bank offices took up the remaining floors. The building had six floors in all, but it was the fourth floor that seemed to get the most attention. The floor was completely vacant. The building's manager was unable to rent it out…to *anyone*, at *any* price. Just stepping off the elevator onto that floor made it clear that *something* was wrong. The temperature was always freezing cold, even in the middle of summer.

Old-timers in the building knew the story and would sometimes tell it to people they felt had been working there long enough. Wallace wasn't told until he'd been there over four years, and then by Monroe.

Supposedly a husband and wife worked in an office on that floor back in 1934. The husband somehow got it into his mind that his wife was having an affair. One day in the office, he shot and killed her and then turned the gun on himself.

Ever since then, the 'happenings' have taken place. You get all the normal stuff – objects moving, strange noises, weird changes in temperature, the feeling of not being alone or of being watched – and a whole lot more. On certain days of the year, that floor of the building would seem to have its own weather, like a fogbank had settled just on it. Sometimes lightning would flash around the building when there was no storm around for miles. And then there was the young worker who decided to bring his tape recorder to the floor. He left it on all day and all night, retrieving it the next day. When he listened to it, he heard about what he expected to – the elevator moving up and down, the drinking fountain's temperature mechanism, creaks in the building…and also the distinct sound of chanting.

That'd thrown everyone at the time, and still did. The young worker had tried to record it again, but it never appeared and soon after he moved on to some other job in some other building in some other town. But for those that remained, the question remained, 'What *was* it?'

Most that knew of the happenings figured it was a satanic cult. But where was it coming from? The building had a basement, but the only access to it was through the first floor of the building, and anyone there would notice a group heading to the basement. Still, there had been whispers over the years of sounds coming from there…almost like someone was trapped down there and desperately trying to get out.

Like most of things in the building, it remained a mystery.

Wallace hadn't known what'd come first – the happenings or the chanting…or what caused either. Did the chanting bring about the crazed state of mind that caused the murder-suicide in '34? Did the murder-suicide somehow create some kind of evil that drew the chanting? Or was there something else that'd caused both?

Wallace had been working at the bank for years, and these things were bothering him. He figured it was a gateway to Hell, perhaps some kind of portal to another plane or dimension or parallel reality. Could even be some kind of subterranean entrance to the hollow earth.

One day he decided to find out.

Letting his manager know he was going to take *a little* longer lunchbreak than usual – "Sorry, Hank, but the wife forgot to pick up the dry cleaning again" – he instead bustled out of the lobby and past the first-floor elevators before the lunch crowd started. His goal was the door to the basement, and he made it without being seen. He grasped the door handle, tested it – unlocked – did a quick double-take with his eyes, and then opened the door and went inside. He shut it quickly but quietly behind him, then leaned up against it and let out a sigh, his heart racing.

Wallace had been thinking of this moment for years. And he knew exactly what to do next.

Lawrence was the building's janitor and all-around maintenance man. Wallace had befriended him enough over the past few months to learn about the crawl space that led even deeper down beneath the bank. If anything satanic or just plain suspicious *was* happening in the bank, then it'd be coming from there…he just knew it.

Looking over his shoulder *just in case*, Wallace moved away from the basement door and toward the far wall, where the crawl space was. He found the spot, moved the few boxes that were covering it, and then lifted the wooden cutout-hatch from the concrete floor. The top of a wooden ladder plunging into the darkness below was all that greeted him.

"Well, here goes," he said as he stood up and turned himself around. He got down on his hands and knees, grasped the floor, put his feet on the ladder, and started down. Before his head passed the lip of the floor, he pulled a flashlight out, turned it on, and pointed it down. About fifteen feet below him was another concrete floor. Clearly, this was a lot more than just a crawl space.

Wallace's heart was racing, but he still kept his head about him. Before he went down any further, he looked about for something to prop the hatch open but could find nothing. The boxes that'd been covering it were cardboard and too flimsy. That's when he got an idea. He reached into his coat pocket and pulled out a pen. It was a fountain pen, not the strongest variety, but it would do in a pinch. The hatch was thrown back but still a bit upright, though held strong by its own weight. Wallace put the pen down where the hatch frame was and went down the ladder.

He was at the concrete floor in seconds. Waving the flashlight about, he saw there was a door at one wall. He started toward it.

That's when he heard the hushed voices above him. It sounded like two people were whispering to each other. Wallace spun around and looked back and up, at the hatch he'd just come through. But there was no one there he could see.

Mind must be playing tricks on me, he thought, and started toward the door again. He reached it, grasped the knob, and found it to be locked.

"Damn," he said under his breath, his thoughts going to Lawrence. Surely the maintenance man would have a key…but how on earth to bring the subject up to him?

Wallace was still pondering that question when he heard the sound again up above him. This time, though, there was also the shuffling of feet.

And then it happened.

The hatch slammed shut…though not all the way. Wallace's pen stopped it from closing completely. He shot his flashlight up to the hatch as it closed and saw it holding there, balancing precipitously on that pen.

Heart racing, Wallace rushed to the ladder and started up. That's when he saw it – a foot. It was covered with a dress shoe and that shoe was moving toward the pen holding the hatch open. It connected, kicking the pen away.

"No!" he shouted, eyes going wide as his hand shot out. The hatch closed completely, his fingers just inches from it. In his haste, he dropped the flashlight. It fell to the concrete floor below and landed just right. The top popped off, the batteries flew out, and just like that, Wallace was plunged into darkness.

No one ever figured out why Wallace had never come back from that *little* longer than usual lunch break to pick up the dry cleaning. In fact, nobody noticed until the next day when his wife called, wondering where he was. Eventually a missing person report was filed with the police. The bank was given a top-down inspection a day later, to no avail.

"Nothing else down here?" the detective had asked Lawrence, the all-around maintenance man, about the basement when the two were down there.

"Just what you see," Lawrence replied, raising his arms up to take the room in, "more cardboard boxes than you can shake a stick at."

The detective nodded, satisfied. In his mind, it was just another disgruntled worker sick with his job, sick of his wife, and ready for a new start somewhere, *anywhere*, else. Not his problem, case closed.

Lawrence led the detective out, back toward the elevators to the first floor. He glanced over his shoulder on the way, looking at the spot where the crawl-space hatch was. Below, Wallace was still down there…slowly starving and dying of thirst. In another day or two he'd be weak enough, offering no resistance. Then he'd be ready for the ceremony.

The all-around maintenance man smiled. He'd done a good job covering the hatch over. Later he'd uncover it enough for the next bored and foolish worker to discover.

The steady stream of human sacrifices would continue.

THE END

18. THE HOUSE AT THE END OF CRAIG LANE

In the small town of Jasper there was a house.

By day the house was white, surrounded by a lush, green yard, and quite ordinary. At night, however, the green light went on. It was a single bulb by the front door, but it washed the whole house in a green glow, one that could be seen nearly a mile away. Suddenly the ordinary daytime house took on an ominous, otherworldly appearance and feel. It was unnatural, and many had commented on that fact over the years.

The owner thought nothing of it, laughed-off such talk. He was Mo Banks, a businessman of sorts that'd moved to the area nearly ten years before. Pinning him down on exactly what he'd done was difficult – sometimes it was in the actuary business, other times banking or investing or even insurance – but there was no denying he had money. He didn't work but was known to spend lavishly at the few restaurants in town. He always drove that year's newest model Oldsmobile. No expense was spared on keeping his lawn looking meticulous.

Most in Jasper found Mo a bit odd and eccentric, but he was a nice-enough man and he sure threw his money around. So they tolerated him, and over time he became just another member of the community.

But still there was talk. It came in hushed voices with one hand over the mouth, but came it did. *He ran away from the big city after killing his wife…was involved in that big savings and loan scandal and had to flee…killed her and her lover…FBI stopped looking for him years ago because he paid 'em to…*

Of course, no one could ever prove any of this…and none of it was ever said to Mo's face. But say it they did, especially when times got hard, like they were this year. It was easy to blame Mo for the town's problems and the townsfolk's lack of money…so they did. Some that did so a lot lately were Nate and Howie's parents.

Both boys were headed to sixth grade in two weeks when summer got out. They'd been dreaming of finally getting to middle school for years now, but now that it was finally happening, they felt a little unsure. So they spent their days outside running about in the nearby woods, playing in the streams, and doing their best to be boys. And like most of the neighborhood kids, that meant a near-constant speculation about the house at the end of Craig Lane.

So it was on this bright and sunny day, Nate and Howie gathered at the end of the lane with their bikes and a few of the neighbor kids. Talk quickly turned to the house's latest victim.

"He got too close at night, it's just that simple," Nate said.

"Bullshit!" Cody shouted, crossing his arms over his chest. The little fourth-grader thought he was a lot tougher than he really was. "The aliens got him, and everyone knows it!"

"Aliens my *ass!*" Doug said with a laugh. He would have been going into sixth grade with Howie and Nate but got held back a year in second.

"Oh yeah, then *what?*" Howie piped-in.

"Same thing that got Old Man Tillet," Cody replied with a smug smile, "the wolves."

Sighs and groans came from the half-dozen kids at that statement.

"That pack of wolves was taken out over *ten years* ago," Nate said with a scoff.

"Oh yeah," Cody shot back, "then what happened to Hank, huh?"

Hank was the latest kid to go missing in Jasper, a kid a few years older than them. For a town so small, there were sure a lot of kids – and people – that just vanished. Over the past decade they'd lost over a dozen that way. Well, not *that* many. Old Man Tillet *had* been half-eaten by the wolves that'd killed him. Then there was that Forest Service worker they figure a bear got. He was so mutilated they had to use dental records. And who could forget the twin girls that'd wandered too far from their campsite a few years ago. They'd been found in a small cave-like outcropping, dead from the elements…even though it'd been summer. And those were just the ones they knew about, knew the cause of death for. The other dozen or so just plain went missing, never to be seen again. That was currently the case with Hank.

"Aliens got him, that's what," one of the younger boys said.

"That's just stupid talk!" Nate shouted out, not even glancing at the boy who'd said it, but instead keeping his eyes on Cody. "Everyone knows Hank's dad is a broke, drunk loser that takes it out on Hank whenever he can." He scoffed. "*That's* where Hank most likely is."

Nate wasn't so sure. Hank's dad hadn't been in town for months. And Nate remembered some other boys mentioning how Hank had wanted to check out the house with the green glow, how he wasn't bothered by the stories. That'd been over a week ago now.

"Well, if it's *so* stupid, they why don't ya'll come back here at night and try what Hank was gonna try for," Cody replied.

Nate rolled his eyes. "Why would I wanna waste my time doing that?"

"What're ya…chicken?"

The other kids went "ooohh" to that, and now it was on. The gauntlet had been thrown down, and Nate wasn't one to just walk away.

"What…you think *I'm* scared?" he said, moving closer to the younger Cody.

"You're a chicken-shit loser," Cody said, moving closer himself.

"Then you're fuckin' on!" Nate shot back. He took in all the kids gathered around then. "Tonight, me and Howie here'll not only *come back*, but we'll get up close and check out that house *real* good."

More "ooohh's" accompanied that, but all Howie could think was, *How the hell'd I get pulled into this?*

~~~

By the time they got back to Craig Lane later that night, none of the other boys had showed.

"I told you so," Howie said. "Now who's gonna see us go near it?"

"Shut up," Nate shot back, then cooled a bit. "Really, when you
~~~

think of it…all we gotta do now is run up real quick, touch the house, and that's it – no one'll know the difference."

"Isn't that all we were gonna do anyways?" Howie asks, but Nate's shrug is all the answer he needs. And really, what did he expect? Of course they'd have had to do more with all the neighbor boys watching. Nate was right – they'd caught a real good break here. Best not to question it.

Next to him, Nate shook his head. "Right. All I'm sayin' is that–"

Nate cutoff midsentence. Ahead of them at the house, the green light had come on.

Howie felt his pulse quicken. A cold chill went through him. His muscles felt watery and his bones stiff. His mouth went dry. What seemed like minutes passed. Then they heard the sound.

WWWwwwRRRrrr…

It was a low-toned 'buzzing' noise coming from…*everywhere!* It was all around, and growing in volume. Howie could feel the hair on his arms beginning to rise. From fear or the sound, he couldn't tell. He wanted to look over at Nate to see if he was experiencing the same, but he couldn't seem to make himself move.

Ahead of them at the house, the green light seemed to pulse, growing a bit fainter before a stronger burst of light came, as if the house itself was a beating heart.

Howie's eyes went wide and it seemed to him that every single hair on his body stood up at once, at least a foot high. Fear coursed through him, and adrenaline too. If it wasn't for that last, he didn't know how he'd have managed to shout out, "Go…run…now!" but somehow he did. He didn't know where the words had come from, but come they had.

He was the first to start running, and he didn't turn around to see if Nate was right behind him or not. A few seconds later he was able to hear a separate set of foot beats besides his own, and besides his own beating heart…which sounded to him like it'd beat right out of his chest.

And then it came – that light. It flashed right behind him. He didn't look back to see – *God, that'd be stupid!* – but he could see its glow on the ground behind him as he peered down at his feet. That meant it was illuminating Nate behind him. He wasn't going to look back to confirm it, though.

They continued on for a few more feet, then the light disappeared as abruptly as it'd appeared. From behind, Nate managed a, "God, it saw me!" as they continued to run.

Howie was now frantic, his breathing intense and his heart racing. He didn't care what happened to Nate anymore – he only cared about saving his own skin. He had no qualms about that, either. Fear had taken hold, driving his primal instincts of survival.

The loud 'wwrring' sound increased behind them, and then an even bigger light illuminated the area around them. Howie could tell it was centered on something behind him, likely Nate. He didn't feel an ounce of guilt in hoping it'd be Nate and not him.

Then the sound of some metal-moving-on-metal, the light increased in intensity, there was another flash from behind, and the scream.

"Aaahhh!" Nate went, but Howie didn't turn to look back. He just kept on running. A moment later the light was gone and a few seconds after that the 'wwrring' sound went away.

But Howie didn't stop running until he was home. He careened into the house and went straight to bed, lying under the covers and shaking with fear until sleep mercifully took him.

~~~

The next morning, Nate's parents came to Howie's house. They were frantic. "Have you seen Nathan," they cried out, desperation clear on their face, tears nearly in their eyes. "We've looked all night and all morning. He…he…he never said a word about going anywhere, with anyone."

All Howie and his parents could do was shake their heads, 'no,' and watch the pair head to another house, hoping those folks had seen something. But deep down, Howie knew they hadn't. He knew that the aliens had taken Nate, just as they suspected might happen. But who could he tell that to? Certainly not Nate's parents. They were frantic enough as it was…adding that kind of fuel to the fire would only make things worse. The police wouldn't care, that's for sure – they'd laugh him out of town. Really…there was no one. No…if he ever wanted to see Nate again, he'd have to get to the bottom of this mystery himself. And that meant heading back to the house at the end of Craig Lane.
~~~

~~~

He went through the rest of the day making plans and keeping to himself. He avoided the other neighbor boys, all of whom wanted to talk about what'd happened to Nate. But Howie already knew. And he knew talking wasn't going to fix what happened.

The only one who could fix it was Mo Banks.

So all that day Howie prepared. Later that night he snuck out of the house, heading toward the house at the end of Craig Lane.

He had his bike helmet on his head, soccer shin guards on his legs, and the old laser tag vest around his torso. He was wearing his thickest hiking boots as well as two pairs of socks. He even put on his long-johns, though it wasn't very cold. He had to be ready.

In his hands he held the ice-breaker his dad sometimes used in the winter. It wasn't much, but it had that sharp metal head on the end. Finally, he had his pocketknife squared away in one pocket.

He kept to the side roads and stayed out of the streetlights. It wasn't long before he was at Craig Lane. It was late and in the distance beyond the trees, he could see that the green light was on.

Something took his best friend, and he meant to find out what. Gripping the ice-breaker tightly, he started down the lane. He didn't know what he expected to do…just hoped something would come to him.

He walked, his heart racing. Past the trees he went and toward the house, then up to it. Fear gripped him, but somehow he made himself move. Or…*something* did.

Then he was at the front door. He watched as his hand went up to the doorbell. He wasn't controlling it, he just knew it, and the hand shook as it slowly moved.

DING-DONG!

It was such a cheery sound for such a scary house, he thought. Then there was the sound of footsteps approaching and the door opened.

A man stood there. He wore pajama pants and an evening jacket. Most of all, Howie noticed how bald he was, with just patches of gray hair on the side of his head. And that head! It was so…*large*. And the eyes, they were large as well.

"Hello Howie," the man said. "I'm Mo Banks. No doubt you're here for Nate."
~~~

Howie's mouth was dry and he couldn't say a word, but somehow found himself nodding. Mo moved away from the door and gestured with his arm for Howie to move inside. He did so, even though he didn't want to. Again that feeling of not really being in control.

"I'm sorry it had to be this way, so…disturbing," Mo said behind him as he closed the door, "but we need new blood, new seed."

Howie did feel a little of control then, and managed to turn around.

"So…so you *are* an alien," Howie said, doing his best to control his fear and keep his voice from shaking.

"No, a hybrid," Mo answers.

"A…*hybrid?*"

"Yes, part-human and part-alien." He shrugs, as if this is all commonplace. "I have no idea who my father was, but I know my mother was human. She was…brought to me a couple times while I was young and growing up." He flinches then, as if the memory pains him. "She never wanted me, thought I was a freak."

Looking at him, Howie could see how people might say that. Now that he was in his own home he wasn't wearing his usual mask or makeup or…whatever he used. Instead his face had much more of an angular appearance, his eyes were a lot bigger, and he just…didn't look human.

"When I was your age, we never knew our fathers because they were alien, and often millions of lightyears away. We were just test-tube babies…but that's all about to change."

Howie narrowed his eyes. *Why is he telling me all this?*

As if reading his mind, Mo smiled and looked back at him. "You see, young man…you'll be like the father I never had." He laughs. "Oh, not to me…but to hundreds – maybe even thousands – of young."

"What do you mean?" Howie says.

"Oh, you're a bit young still, but in a couple years you'll be the prime age for child-rearing. And that's what you – and your friend Nate – will be used for, hooked up to the 'milkers' to make lots and lots of beautiful hybrid babies."

As if to accentuate the truth of his words, a strange 'humming' noise could be heard off in the distance, though it really did sound like it was coming from all around. It grew in volume, and after a moment Mo smiled.

"They're here."

Mo moved over to one window, pulled the curtains aside, and there in the yard was a large UFO. It sat on three legs, and a hatch was already open, a walkway extending down from it. Two large gray aliens walked down it, carrying some strange pieces of equipment. They walk to the house and then right *through* the front door, as if it wasn't closed and wasn't even there.

No words were exchanged between them and Mo as they came into the room, but Howie got the distinct impression that they were communicating, most likely telepathically. Then the two aliens started toward him. He tried to fight and kick, but still couldn't move.

The aliens took their cases and set them down. One opened their case, pulled some kind of small metal object out, and pointed it at Howie.

Everything went black.

~~~

He didn't know how long he'd been out by the time he woke up, but he knew he was in a different place. He was in a strange kind of room, equipment all around him, tubes of all kinds running from his body, even from his mouth. He was on some kind of bed, and a quick glance to one side revealed there were dozens more beds like his, each with a boy like him on it, all looking as panicked as he felt.

And all Howie could think was how much he'd wish he'd stayed away from that green light, wished he'd stayed away from the house at the end of Craig Lane.

THE END
~~~

19. AN EVIL KNIFE

Carl headed out on the stoop and groaned. Another beautiful day and he was stuck…*here.* The asphalt jungle, the big city, concrete everywhere. And it'd likely be this way all summer, too, Carl thought…*stuck inside with nowhere to go, and no way to get there if there* was *someplace.*

"Hey!"

Carl spun around. It was Tanner from upstairs.

"Wanna head over to White Lake Park?"

Carl shrugged. "Got nothin' else to do."

Tanner smiled and ruffled Carl's hair as he got into the Jeep. "I knew you didn't."

~~~

On the way over to the lake they mostly listened to the radio. Carl had just turned 13 and Tanner was somewhere in his 30s. They didn't have a whole lot in common, but Tanner couldn't help trying to get the typically shy and quiet Carl to talk. He started by asking about school, friends…always something to needle his way to the subject of his mom.

"She's fine," Carl said.

"Didn't sound fine last night," Tanner replied just as tersely.

And with that, the conversation ended and the oldies station took over.

Carl sighed. Tanner was just trying to help. He often heard the
~~~

drunken fights downstairs, and sometimes even came to break them up. Well...*tried* to. A couple times he'd gotten a black eye because of it.

Carl had never known another way of living. If it wasn't Tanner trying to save him and his mom, it was some other neighbor in some other city in some other state. That's how he'd always grown up.

For as long as he could remember, he'd been a shy loner. It was just easier that way. I mean...*what?* Bring friends over to see mom beaten-up between episodes of *Saved By the Bell*...sleepovers to hear her get raped? No thanks.

It was no secret around school that Carl's homelife was troubled, but he was able to keep it to just that...for now. At other schools, he hadn't been so lucky. That's usually when he and mom would move, try and start over somewhere else. It never lasted more than a week or two.

Janet was Carl's waitress mom and she'd inevitably find some biker-type that used her for sex and little else. And those were the good ones. Carl's dad was long gone. He'd always been raised by a single mother that'd been beaten by too many boyfriends for Carl to count. He often tried to get out of the house, escaping to nature. At least then he didn't have to listen to his mom doing her OnlyFans shows online. But then he had to tell himself what he always did – she has to make end's meat.

The latest 'winner' that she'd found was named Eddie. He was a tattooed hoodlum that made white trash look bad. Long, greasy black hair was tied back behind his head, and he wore a motorcycle gang jacket over his white tank-top, despite never having been in a motorcycle gang. He was Janet's latest boyfriend, a worker at a local shipping warehouse. He drank too much, hated his lot in life, and took it out on Janet every chance he got.

The thoughts faded as they neared the lake. White Lake was just a few miles around, but it was deep and made for good fishing and boating. There was a lot of that on this hot day, and by the time they drove halfway around the lake to the state park they'd seen dozens of other cars, people out and having fun under the sun.

"There's a spot," Tanner said, pointing toward the parking lot away from the lake. They pulled-in, got out, and were soon at lake's edge. They took in the placid nature of the place, wonderful green trees reflecting from the water's surface, which was sparkling with a million diamond-shaped bursts from the dazzling sun above.

"Hey! Hey, Carl!"

Carl and Tanner both spun around. After a few moments, Carl was able to make out his friend Bud. Bud was Carl's best friend…if you want to call it that. He was more of a bully to Carl, but Carl was just happy to have someone to talk to.

"Hey, I didn't know you'd be here today," Bud says, panting a bit from running up to them. "Wanna hang out."

Carl looked over at Tanner, who nodded. "I'll be over by the picnic tables, just relaxing," he said. Carl nodded back and then he and Bud were off, running to the lake's edge and then all around it. It was a busy day at the lake, with people all around. The boys had to get off the beaten path to find some privacy, and to not bother the many families with their loud horseplay. It was then that Carl caught sight of it.

"Hey…what's that!"

Both boys stopped, but Carl was closer to the flash of light that'd caught their eye. He narrowed his eyes and put his hand up to block out the sun…but not before it caught something and gave off that flash again. That's how he saw it – a knife!

He dashed forward before Bud could beat him, reaching out for it. The knife had a gold-plated handle with silver inlay, and the blade was sticking out from it, a shiny silver that looked freshly polished. Carl's hand went for it and grasped hold. It felt good in his hand, warm from the sun and just…*right*.

"Let me see it!" Bud called from behind him, disappointment in his voice that *he* wasn't the one to find it first.

"It's mine, I found it first," Carl replied, holding the knife up before him. It was a shiny blade, with a hard, plastic-metal composite for the handle, he saw now. A push button allowed the blade to fold closed. Carl fumbled with that part.

"Here, let me do it!" Bud shouted, reaching for the knife, but Carl was faster and shouldered out of the way, spinning so his back was to Bud. "You've got to push the button, you dumbass!"

Carl felt his face going red, for he'd had no idea how to get the knife closed. The truth was…he'd never really handled a knife before, at least nothing more than the kitchen variety that mom kept in the drawer, and those weren't much more than butter knives, even the serrated ones. He'd certainly never seen anything as exquisite as this knife, and that's what it was to him – exquisite. Oh, he'd seen knives like this before – he and one of his mom's old boyfriends stared at them in the case at Walmart on those rare times when they were being nice to him – but he'd never actually held one. And now…one of them was his, all his!

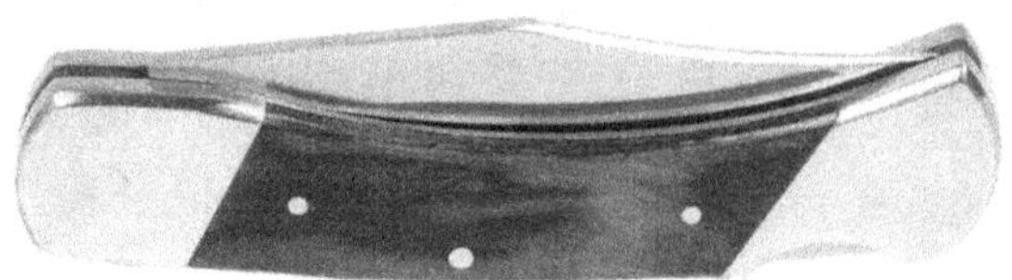

"Just let me see it!" Bud said again, reaching.

"It's mine," Carl said, spinning back around to confront his friend. "I found it and I'm keeping it."

Bud frowned and crossed his arms over his chest. "Well, fine then! I didn't want the damn thing anyways. It's ugly, and dirty, and it's not even sharp anyways. Plus, I've got too many *ugly* knives at home to deal with now as it is. In fact, I was planning on throwing a few away."

"You should probably go do that, then," Carl said, not really listening as he continued to stare at the knife. He couldn't really describe what the feeling was that had come over him. It wasn't like the knife was anything that special – just your typical store-bought cheapo knife. But he couldn't stop staring at it…or more rightly, *into* it.

"Ya gonna make out with it, too?" Bud quipped with a laugh. "Keep it all nice and close to you tonight in bed? Maybe rub it a little against–"

"Shut the fuck up!" Carl said, spinning around on Bud.

"O…okay, man – just cool it!" Bud said, more quietly this time, his hands now up in front of him. It was then that Carl noticed that a knife was pressed up against Bud's throat, *his* knife, the one he'd just found…and he was the one holding it. Not knowing what had come over him, he quickly pulled the knife back.

"S-…sorry," he stammered, staring down at the blade. It caught a glint of sunlight and flashed a blinding light into his eyes for just a split-second. For some weird reason, he thought the knife was smiling at him.

"Man, screw you!" Bud said, turning to run away. He made it to his bike, grabbed it, and was soon peddling away, every once in a while giving a cold look over his shoulder back at Carl.

Carl watched him go, shrugged, then looked back down at the knife. Time to go home, he thought.

~~~

They'd stayed at the lake for another hour or so then Tanner said they had to get back to the city. Carl barely remembered the drive, so intent was he on the knife. He vaguely remembered Tanner asking him about it a few times, but he'd mostly shrugged off the questions, giving one-word answers. He just didn't feel like talking.

They got home as dusk was approaching, which was good – Carl's mom would still be working and Eddie would be at the bar for another couple hours, too. He had the whole place to himself! After saying 'thanks' and 'bye' to Tanner, he headed into his apartment and then his room. He threw his things on his bed, sat down at his desk, and took out the knife. He just wanted to…*stare at it.*

It was as if the knife knew all his problems…all his hopes and fears and dreams…and wanted to help him. Sometimes, if he cocked his head just right, Carl swore he could hear the knife…*speaking to him.*

BANG!

Carl spun around in his chair at the sound of the front door slamming closed. A moment later he could hear two voices.

"So's I tell the fuckin' bitch, 'Man, bitch, you better shut the fuck up or I'm gonna knock you into the middle of next week!'"

"What'd she say to that?"

There was a laugh. "Dumb broad didn't say nothin' – she was too busy haulin' ass outta there!"

The living room was soon full of guffawing laughter, which meant only one thing – Eddie was home, and worse…he'd brought Sid with him. Sid was Eddie's best bud, drinking pal, and all around sleazeball. He laughs when Eddie hits Janet and Carl, and dreams of having sex with Janet on those common occasions when Eddie passes out early. Of course, sex with Carl would be just as good.

Carl let out a sigh and rolled his eyes. Most nights started just like this – Eddie coming home half-drunk, ready to pound a few more
~~~

then beat on Carl and his mom…if he didn't just pass out first. And by the sound of it, tonight would be a night when he'd stay up late…making for a fight.

Carl started to get up from his desk, the usual feeling of dread and hopelessness coming over him. But then…it did something it'd never done before – it stopped. For some reason, the helpless feeling that usually took hold of Carl this time of night was replaced by…anger. That's when Carl noticed how tightly he was gripping the knife, so much so that his knuckles had turned white.

"Carl…Carl – you home, you little shit!" The shout came from Eddie in the living room, quickly followed by his laughter and then Sid's. "Get out here, boy! I got somethin' I wanna say to you!"

Inside his room, Carl sighed and made for the door. There was no point in making Eddie wait; no point in making him anymore angry. He opened it, headed out into the short hallway, and then the living room. There were Eddie and Sid, both sitting on the couch with their bottles of Miller Hi-Life open, a bottle of Jim Beam nearby.

"Boy, what the hell you been doin' all day, huh?" Eddie said quickly, before Carl even had a chance to say 'Hi.' He could tell from the tone of his voice that Eddie was both drunk and angry. "Didn't I tell you last night that I wanted this place cleaned up?"

Carl looked around. Besides a few magazines lying on the coffee table, the place was spick and span. He shrugged and looked back at Eddie. "It's already clean."

"Then what the hell is *that*?!" Eddie nearly screamed as he brought his arm up and threw his nearly empty bottle of beer at the wall. It shattered, sending bits of glass and drops of beer flying everywhere.

Silence fell in the room, but only for a moment. Then Sid started that grating laugh of his, quickly joined by Eddie. Carl just gave an inward groan but kept silent. He'd talked-back after something like this before. It never ended well. Instead he just headed to the small closet by the front door, grabbed the broom and dustpan, and started sweeping. After a minute he'd gotten it all.

"You missed a piece," Eddie said as he started to flip through the channels on the TV, looking for some kind of sports game to watch.

"So what," Carl said under his breath.

"What was that?" Eddie said, shooting up from his spot on the couch. "What the fuck did you just say?"

"N…nothing," Carl replies, already wishing he'd have just kept his mouth shut. But it was too late. Eddie rushed across the room to him and shoved him hard. The force of it sent Carl down to the floor.

"Ow, that hurt!" Carl said, though he immediately regretted it. Eddie loved causing pain, and if he knew he had and that it bothered you, he'd try to cause more.

He sneered down at Carl. "What the hell ya gonna do about it, boy?"

The sneer turned to a smirk, and then Eddie started to laugh, that jagged cackle of his that was like a nailfile going down Carl's spine. A deep anger welled-up inside him, and without knowing it, he began balling his fists at his sides. Above him, Eddie was still laughing, but now turning his attention to Sid on the couch. At first Sid looked concerned – Carl had fallen hard to the floor after Eddie's shove – but at one look from his friend, he knew better than to look anything but supportive. He too was soon laughing, pointing his fingers there at Carl on the floor. More anger rose up, and a warmth started in Carl's pocket. That warmth grew to a hotness, a hotness that matched the anger building in him.

Without warning, Carl lunged up from his position on the floor, his hands balled into fists and aiming strait for Eddie's face. Eddie was caught off guard, still half-looking over at Sid. He was only able to move away a fraction, catching most of Carl's fist right on the edge of his eye. Carl's other fist missed completely, throwing him off balance. But Eddie was now off balance as well. Sid just sat on the couch, perplexed and muttering, "Holy shit!"

Carl's anger – and the bloodlust of the knife in his pocket – wouldn't allow him to remain off-balance for long. With a few quick steps, he righted himself, spun about, and brought the fist that'd missed back around at Eddie's face.

BOP!

Right in the cheek! That one stunned the hell out of him, Carl saw, but it didn't really do much damage. A second later, Eddie was turning his face back to him, anger flashing in his eyes.

"You little shit!" he spat, and lunged toward Carl, both of his hands out and reaching for the boy's throat.

Carl dodged out of the way, and while doing so, reached into his pocket. He pulled the knife out just as Eddie was flying past him. Somehow, the knife opened on its own. Then it was shooting out at

Eddie. It struck him in the side and stayed there as Eddie's lunge propelled him forward. By the time he was past, he had a bloody streak several inches down his torso.

"The fuck!?!" Eddie says, fingering the gash at his side. His hand comes back covered in blood, and he sets a look of hate on Carl before turning to rush back at him. But Carl is ready and brings the knife up. Eddie propels himself right into the blade, taking it in the chest. He gives a dumbfounded look at the thing sticking from him, then Carl pulls it out and blood flies. Eddie gives one more confused look before crumpling to the floor, dead.

"Holy shit!" Sid says from his spot on the couch. "What the fuck'd you do?"

Carl just clenches the knife more tightly, and anger and rage rush into him. Without giving Sid another chance to talk, Carl lunges for him on the couch.

"Aahh!!!" Sid yells as the knife tears into his throat.

A fountain of blood sprays against the wall, but Carl doesn't stop, feeling as though he's possessed, and continues to stab and swipe with the knife until Sid is just a bloody, unmoving mess. Then he got up, his heart nearly beating from his chest. He stood staring down at the two bodies on the floor, blood splattered all over the place. *What am I gonna do?* he thought to himself, but those thoughts were interrupted by pounding at the door.

"Carl…Janet – you alright?!?"

It was Tanner from upstairs. Carl couldn't let him see the place like this, not before he cleaned up. He just had to–

Before he could do anything, the door opened. Eddie had never locked it and Carl hadn't had time to. Tanner got two steps into the place before he froze, eyes wide. He took in the grisly scene, then looked at Carl.

"What…what happened?"

"Here, take it," Carl says, pushing the knife into Tanner's hand before the man can say anything else.

"No, I don't–" Tanner started to say, but stopped once the metal touched his hand. At that point, a strange sensation seemed to come over him, Carl noticed. He took on a calmer appearance and much of the worry seemed to drain from face. He looked down at the knife…and smiled.

"It's…there's something *wrong* with that knife," Carl managed to say before Tanner looked up at him. He knew right away that there was now something wrong with Tanner. He took a step back, then seeing the strange glint in his neighbor's eye, he took another. Tanner noticed and gave a strange smile…an evil smile.

"What's the matter, Carl…'fraid you might get in trouble for all the…mayhem you've caused?"

"Just…just go," Carl says, backing away further. In front of him, Tanner brings the knife up to chest height as he started to step toward Carl, that sinister smile on his lips.

"I will, just let me give you a little something first," Tanner says before lunging at Carl. The knife thrusts forward so quickly that Carl can do little more than twist to one side, but it's not enough. The knife bites into his torso, is gone, and then bites again.

"Aaahhh!" Carl screams as the knife bites again. In front of him, Tanner has a possessed look in his eyes and a maniacal smile on his face. He stabs and stabs and stabs…until Carl is lying on the floor at his feet, a bloody mess that doesn't move.

Tanner looks at his handiwork and smiles. He looks down at the knife in his hand, and smiles even more. Somehow, the knife is speaking to him, telling him how good he is, how happy it is with him. A sudden urge to kiss the knife comes over Tanner. He brings it to his face and licks the blood from the blade.

"Oh…my…God!"

Tanner spins around to see Janet standing there in the doorway, a look of shock and bewilderment on her face. Her eyes are wide at the scene of blood and bodies, and grow wider still as she focuses on Tanner standing there with the knife in his hand looking at her.

Tanner smiles, the blood still on his lips. He brings the knife up and starts moving toward Janet.

"No…No…*NO!!!*" she screams.

THE END

20. LOOTING ANIVA LIGHTHOUSE

It was cold and foggy and Peter wanted to be anywhere else. But there was nowhere else for him to go. He'd reached the end of the line. His money was spent. He had nothing. Worse…he owed. And with *his* kind of debts, it'd be his family that paid if he didn't…and not in the good way, but the kind of way that left them maimed or crippled or dead.

That's why Peter was here, in the cold and the fog on the edge of the world.

It was Sakhalin, the island that Russia didn't really want, and Japan either. No one wanted it, and few of the half million people that called it home wanted it, either. But they were there and had to make the best of it…which was damn-near impossible these days. *Was it even this bad in Soviet times…or shortly after the fall?*

Peter sighed. *No use in worrying on what I can't do anything about,* he thought, and returned his gaze to the task at hand.

For hours now they'd been on the boat, the rough seas making what should have been a simple two-hour journey into nearly five hours already. But at least they were there. Peter turned and looked back at Victor behind him. They'd grown up together, gotten into trouble together, and now Peter hoped, they'd find a way to get out of it together. Victor looked up then, gave a slight smile at Peter, but then nodded over his shoulder. Peter turned back to look out the front of the boat…and there it was – Aniva Lighthouse.

Peter got his first good look at the light. She stood over thirty meters tall, jutting up from the sharp rocks that dotted that section of coast, though the light itself was another ten meters above that. The water churned violent and angry below. The lighthouse was almost like two different designs had competed on the architect's table. The bottom base section was round and made of stone. The upper portion was half the circumference of what came below, and that mostly constructed of concrete. Above it was the metal walkway with metal fencing all around, the outside of the massive light…which sat idle and uncaring, not used in over fifteen years.

Excited chatter could be heard from the small captain's cabin at the front of the fishing boat, and a few moments later, the first mate burst forth, a smile on his face.

"We're here," he said, motioning back toward the front of the boat and the light that was still half a mile from them.

Peter nodded and behind him, Victor began to put his book away. In front of them, the first mate continued. "We'll get as close as we can to the shore, but there are no guarantees…like we said."

Peter nodded at him, and with that, the man headed back into the cabin to help the captain get the boat into position. Peter hoped they would at least get them onto the rock with the light, not the headlands dozens of feet from it. The seas were just too rough to try for a swim, even one as short as that. *They damn well better get us on it, what with all the money I've paid!* Peter thought to himself as the boat began a series of subtle turns, the better to get it into some kind of docking or at least landing position. It was the only boat that Peter could find to take them from Nadhodka to the light, which usually only saw visitors during the warmer summer months, when the seas weren't so angry. And those were all specially designed tourist boats, craft meant to land on these jagged rocks and depart again. Peter was on a common fishing boat now, and there was no guarantee he'd make it to shore. And that turned out to be the case.

"We can't make it to shore," the first mate said as he came back out of the cabin, shaking his head and putting on his best look of distress and sorrow.

"How about another ten thousand rubles," Peter said.

"The rocks, the waves…" the man shook his head, "Captain says—"

"Twenty thousand," Peter replies, cutting him off while pulling out the bills to wave in the air.

"I don't think the sea's as bad as the captain thinks," the first mate said, snatching the money from Peter's hand as he turned and headed back into the cabin. A minute later, they were moving closer to the rocks of the lighthouse. Peter and Victor exchanged a smiling look.

Minutes later the two men were on deck, a stiff rain pelting them as they stood at the railing.

"This is it!" Victor shouted over the sound of the waves and the wind and rain.

Peter nodded, grasped his bag tightly to his chest, and then jumped over the side. He landed in the waves, his feet hitting the sandy and rocky bottom. He was drenched up to his waist and immediately started moving toward the shore. A splash to his rear told him that Victor was right behind. A few moments later the sound of the boat's engines could be heard roaring to life. Peter turned to see the boat turning away. Victor looked back at him with concern.

"It's alright – they're just going to head further out, away from the waves and any chance of getting beached here."

Victor nodded to the words and the two men continued through the water. Peter hoped what he had said proved to be true. It was part of the deal – thirty thousand for a safe ride to Aniva *and back*. He just hoped the first mate and the captain didn't forget that last part.

Kicking those thoughts from his head, Peter and Victor continued on, made it out of the waves, kicked some water out of their shoes on the beach, and then headed for the concrete pedestal that held the lighthouse.

A stairway had been carved into the rocks years before, and soon the two men were moving up it, twisting around the base of the light as they made their ascent. Seagulls cawing was the only sound they could hear above the crashing of the waves.

The two men moved in silence up the rocky steps, each taking their time and finding the proper foothold. One slip here would mean a tumble of dozens of feet down to the sharp rocks below, and if not a certain death, then at least enough broken bones to make you wish it.

Peter shook those thoughts from his head. Death really had no meaning for him anymore, not after the latest diagnosis from the doctor. Perhaps a quick fall would be better than months of slow agony. And of course, that was one of the main reasons why Peter had decided now was the time – he had nothing left to lose. If he could find what he was looking for – and what rightfully shouldn't even be there any longer – then he could live out his remaining days a rich man. Better yet, he could make sure his mother and sister lived out their days the same way. *It's the least I can do…after all I've put them through.*

It was slow-going up the wet and slippery steps dug into the sides of the rock. Above them the seagulls squawked and cried, while below the rhythm of waves crashing on rocks gave them a steady beat to keep time to. The men's attention was mostly on the faint path in front of them, making sure each step was good and wouldn't send them plummeting. But they still had time to take in the scenery, which was dominated by the large lighthouse.

The light had been built to protect ships from Cape Aniva. The Japs had started construction in 1937 and after two grueling years, finished in 1939. Construction was nearly impossible at time due to the elements, and the difficulty in getting materials to the site. The choppy waters took more than one supply boat down to the depths in the process.

Peter had studied the blueprints meticulously to ensure he didn't miss a single hiding spot. The light, nine floors in all, was designed as both a beacon and a home. Its basement had diesel engines and batteries for a constant supply of power, no matter the conditions. The kitchen and food pantries could be found on the ground floor, and above them on the second were the radio, equipment, and watch rooms. The third, fourth, and fifth floors were all taken up by living quarters, enough space to house twelve men to have their own rooms. Small porthole windows in each would offer enough illumination to see the two bunk beds and small alcoves for personal items in each. The storeroom was on the sixth floor, the seventh had the pneumatic siren mechanisms that controlled the large horn on the light's roof, while the eighth floor was reserved for fuel storage. That left only the ninth, which was where the light itself resided in a large bowl of 300 kg of mercury. The light was rotated by a 270 kg weight that was suspended from the spiral staircase that went from the top floor to the bottom. It took that weight three hours to lower itself to the ground floor, whereupon the keeper would have to rewind it so it could begin again. Doing so allowed the light to rotate out over 17 miles into the open sea.

It was several years after the Japs had invaded China, and just two years before they struck the Americans at Pearl Harbor, effectively launching the Second World War. By that time, the Russians hated the Japanese, had for decades. Sakhalin Island had always been a part of Russia…that is, until the Japs had won it in the Russo-Japanese war of 1905. The Japs had hoped it'd become part of their Pacific empire, but instead they'd lost and the island reverted back to Russia.

Not that it was wanted, by then. Seen more of a burden than a blessing, the light fell into disuse, with one drunken keeper after another tending to it until the year 1990, when the last keeper was let go. From that point on, Aniva Lighthouse would be nuclear, with a nuclear core for power.

The proper term was RTG, or radioisotope thermoelectric generator. It was a type of nuclear battery that converted the heat released by the decay of the radioactive isotope to electricity, thus creating power for things like a satellite, space probe, or a lighthouse light. They worked great in isolated areas that needed little relative power but couldn't get it from solar or conventional connection methods. The RTG's would last for nearly 90 years before decay inhibited any substantial power production. And the good news for Peter was that they were relatively small, about three feet tall and a foot wide…easy enough for one person to move by themselves. That was their plan.

Aniva Lighthouse continued on like that, solitary and alone with just the isotopic radiation to power her and keep her company. Sixteen long years passed, and then in 2006 the Russian government decided that the light was no longer needed, the isotope installations were removed, and the light was abandoned to the elements…and the looters.

They were few at first, fearing any leftover radiation that might still exist. But then the first few brave ones came, took what treasures they could find, and word spread. Within a couple years, not much was left in the lighthouse of value. The looters stopped coming for the most part, and Aniva fell to the birds.

But there were always stories…stories of some isotopes being missed, perhaps even some buried treasure from the Japanese days. It was those isotopes that Peter was interested in, though. Their value on the black market would prove immense, possibly running into the millions of rubles…if he could find the right buyer. *And if I can even get the damn thing out*, he thought.

Peter and Victor continued on up the rocky steps, the lighthouse growing larger with each approaching step. It wouldn't be long now.

And then they were there, above the base and at the actual light itself. A few more feet brought them to the heavy iron door, a chain and padlock plain to see. Peter moved closer to inspect.

"It's just a flimsy lock keeping the front door closed," Victor said next to him after a few moments, breaking Peter from his reverie. "Lock cutters'll make short work of 'er."

Peter nodded. "Then let's get to it."

Victor moved forward, took the pack off his back, and pulled a pair of bolt cutters out. A moment later, the lock was lying broken at their feet. Next he removed the chain, gave a look back at Peter, and then made to pull the door open. It was tough, though, and he couldn't do it alone. Peter came up and they both grabbed hold of the metal handle and pulled as hard as they could. Nothing at first…then it began to budge…and then…

WOOSH!

A blast of hot, fetid air rushed out at them as they managed to jerk the door open, probably the first time it'd done so in years. Both men had to turn and cough.

"Ugh, what *is* that!" Victor said as Peter continued to gasp.

"I…dunno…" Peter managed as he made to catch his breath, "but it's awful."

"And it's all you, now," Victor replied. "You still want to do this alone?"

Peter nodded. The plan had been for him to go in alone, find the core, and get it out. There were lots of stories of Aniva Lighthouse being full of radiation from the cores, but they were just that — stories. Still, the two weren't taking any chances. Peter would go in while Victor waited outside. He'd get the core, quickly wrap it in the special X-ray vest they'd gotten online, and then make haste back to the door. From there, the two men would ferry the heavy core down the steps and back to the boat, where they'd put it in a special cooler that they'd personally lined with lead plates. Hopefully that would be enough to keep them safe from whatever radiation still existed…at least long enough to sell the thing to the highest bidder and retire to some island paradise.

"Good luck" Victor said as Peter headed into the lighthouse. Behind him, Victor put a wooden doorstop down to keep the large door propped-open and fresh air moving in.

Inside, the interior was a mess. It was the ground floor and wires and bits of wood lay all about, straw covering the floor in some spots, bird feathers in others. All of the furniture that was still left — mostly tables, some chairs, shelving — was rusted and broken. Every window had been broken out as well. *Strange,* Peter thought, as this would have allowed fresh air in, but the whole place smelled dead and rotten. It wasn't a good smell and it wasn't a good sight. Peter located the circular stairway to the upper levels and began to move up it.

He passed up and through the radio room, then the three floors of living quarters. Each was ramshackle, metal-framed beds rusting away in mountains of trash and debris. Upward he went, past the storeroom level then the siren level and fuel storage level. Finally he was at the top, the floor with the light itself. Wind hit him immediately from the broken-out windows. All about him were radioactive warning signs, the first he'd seen. He knew he was in the right place.

And then he saw it. There before him was the core, the RTG. It was smaller than he expected, about two feet high instead of three, and not even a foot wide. *The easier to move it,* he thought as he stepped closer. All around it was rubble and rust, but for some reason, the generator core looked like it hadn't been touched since the day it'd been installed sixteen years before. With a smile on his face, Peter moved forward, his arms outstretched to grasp the core. It was still warm! Quickly, he reached down and began to undo the few wires and cords running into the thing. Then he grabbed hold and jerked. The RTG came loose from its housing on the floor and was in his arms, heavy…but manageable.

BOOM!

A deafening crash from the direction he'd come. Peter didn't have to see it to know what it was – the huge lighthouse door had slammed shut. For the first time, panic began to seep into his bones. It filled his mind, cutting off all rational thought…for a moment. Quickly, he regained his composure, gritted his teeth, and set the RTG back down. He took off his pack, retrieved the X-ray covering, and wrapped it around the core as best he could. Then he took it up once again and started back down the circular staircase.

Immediately he knew that something had changed. The air felt different. The seagulls weren't squawking. Even the wind and waves seemed to have died down. Suddenly, out of the corner of his eye, Peter saw a flash of light.

"What the hell…?"

Then he saw it again, that quick flash of whiteness, not light so much and not movement, either. It just *was*…he couldn't put it any other way. And it wasn't just seeing things, either. Something was here in this light with him, he knew it…could *feel* it.

Fear crept into him then, and Peter began to rush down the steps, not really caring if he hurt himself or damaged the core. He had an overwhelming need to get out of there, now! At one turn in the stairs, just below the fourth floor, he glanced out the broken-out window and stopped dead in his tracks. The view was clear down to the jagged rocks at the bottom of the light's pedestal base. There, in a pool of blood, was Victor. It was as if he'd fallen from the base all the way down to the rocks thirty feet below.

What could have done that? Peter thought as he scrambled down the stairs, his arms aching from carrying the heavy nuclear generator. *No wind is strong enough to blow a man that far!*

"Maybe…" Peter began to say, thinking the first mate back on the boat might have seen something, might be coming to check. But no…the boat was nowhere to be seen, nowhere at all!

"Gone!" Peter shouted, desperation creeping into his voice. Then he saw it again.

Peter was just a dozen steps from the bottom when that quick flash reappeared, then became a steady image. He froze mid-step, and the blood inside him seemed to do the same. Every hair on his body stood up, and the pins and needles sensation of fear rippled across every inch of his skin. There before him, staring straight at him, was what he could only describe as a ghost.

It was a woman, probably in her thirties. Face smudged with dirt, clothes disheveled, and eyes that seemed to hold every bit of sadness in the world. But that wasn't what was odd. No…she seemed to have a faint, translucent hue to her…like she wasn't *really there*. Her coloring was drab as well, like it was all greyed-out.

Somehow Peter knew her whole story, though he had no idea how. She was just like him, a struggling worker in Vladivostok that had fallen on hard times, lost hope, and decided there was one last thing to try. She'd tried it…and failed. The nuclear generator she'd tried to get out had killed her. Peter knew now that it would kill him, too.

Frantically he rushed past the 'girl,' dropping the generator as he did so. It no longer mattered to him. He reached the door, started pulling on it, but he knew he couldn't move it by himself. He was trapped. Tears welling-up in his eyes, Peter turned his back to the door and slowly let himself sink down to the floor.

Staring back at him was that ghostly girl…and this time others, others like him…the lost and the desperate, the youth of Russia that wanted so much more from life…and paid a terrible price trying to get it.

THE END

21. MOVING DAY

Bill Beck stared at the lighthouse on the tiny island. He hoped he didn't see any ghosts while he was there.

He chuckled to himself at the thought. Although Seguin Island Light Station had a bit of bad history associated with it, no one had ever seen any ghosts. That bad bit from the 1850s was long forgotten, and the only ones that told the tale anymore were people in the Maine department of the U.S. Coast Guard that wanted to scare some of the new recruits.

Bill was long past his scaring days, though, and his coworkers knew it. Just a few years shy of retirement, Bill typically got the plumb jobs...like the one he was on now. It consisted of taking out the old acetylene gas lights atop the house and putting in a new Fresnel lens.

The light itself had been standing since 1795. George Washington commissioned its construction after Massachusetts ceded 10 acres of land to the federal government for the task. Originally the light was built of wood, but in 1817 Congress gave enough money to replace it with stone.

Bill knew the stories of the place well, the incident that'd happened over 130 years before. The original keeper had killed his wife in a fit of insane rage.

Still, the light had been there ever since and there'd been dozens of keepers in that time.

The first was Major John Polereczky in 1796. He kept the light working for five years at a pay of $150 a year. The keepers came and went as the years went on. Then in 1939 the U.S. Coast Guard took command of the light. A few years later, the last of the civilian keepers left. The light kept on like that for another four decades, under the watchful eyes of the Coast Guard men that manned it.

But now even that was coming to an end. It was 1985 and the government had decided that now was the time to automate the light. So the old lenses would go and the new battery-powered and operated type would go in. It was the end of an era for this corner of Maine, and Bill knew it.

So it was that Bill and his small crew were chosen to decommission the light. The waves and surf bobbed their small boat about, but in time they made it to shore and were soon going up the steep hillsides to get to the light.

It was early morning when they started, but by lunch Bill's three-man crew had completely disassembled the old gas light, hauled it down the fifty feet of stairs, and gotten it into the boat and to the mainland. They were all surprised how easy the job was, how fast they'd completed it. It was supposed to be a two-day job with the light, but now they had time to do a secondary task – remove all the old furniture that'd been sitting there since the last keeper left in the 1940s.

Much of it dated to much older times than that, and quite a few of the pieces could be called antiques. The Coast Guard wanted it all sold off, hoping to get a few more dollars to supplement that year's meager budget.

So the men got to it, moving up and down the stairs for hours as they grabbed each chair, desk, table, sofa, and every other piece of furniture in sight. It was more work than it looked, mainly because just two men were doing it after the first load was brought down. The other two boated the stuff to the mainland, coming back for another load an hour or so later. Dusk was approaching as they loaded the last few pieces into the boat.

"She's full, sir," one of the men said to Bill as the four of them stood on the dock.

Bill scanned the boat and nodded, more to the meaning behind the man's words than the words themselves. "And it'll be too dark to do another run." He gave an inward sigh as he looked back up at the lighthouse, then turned back to the man.

"Don't worry about me," Bill said with a nod, seeing where this was going, "I'll be fine here 'till morning."

"Aye," the worker replied, turning back to the boat and the other three men standing there, ready to go. Within minutes they were in the surf and heading back to the mainland. Bill was left standing on the dock, a night in the lighthouse before him.

He didn't want to, but Bill also knew it didn't make a lot of sense heading back to the mainland. The journey itself would take at least an hour in this high tide, then he'd have to get in the car, drive all the way to Portland, and then repeat the process in reverse the next morning…which was only hours from now.

No, Bill thought to himself, *it just wouldn't be worth it.* So it was a night at the light, either inside or out. One look up at the sky and how it was going to storm told him the latter was out of the question. So inside it was.

As far as he knew, no one had stayed at Sequin Light since 1942…forty-three years before. Nothing happened to them, and no stories of ghosts were ever told.

Bill rolled his eyes at the thought of ghosts as he climbed up the staircase leading to the third-floor bedrooms. It wasn't the main bedroom – that was on the fourth floor – but it was a guest room and it still had a bed and other furnishings. Those would be gone come morning. Bill and a couple hired hands from town would move them to the dock, load them on a boat, and get them to the mainland. From there the items would be sold, the proceeds going to the Maine Coast Guard account.

Darkness was coming on, but Bill wasn't quite ready for bed just yet. He decided to do a bit more work around the place. The windows were cleaned, their sills scrubbed. The kitchen was cleaned out, probably for the first time in decades. Finally, he was tired and ready for bed.

If he was honest with himself, Bill would have said he'd cleaned and tidied up to keep himself from bed as long as possible. He had a bad feeling about sleeping in the place, much more so than just a couple hours earlier on the dock.

And then the rain came. It started slowly, pattering against the windows of the light, but then harder, banging its discontent. Lightning and thunder soon followed. Bill did his best to ignore it as he got ready for bed, finally lying himself down in the last remaining bed. Sleep took him quickly.

He didn't know how long he slept but a peal of thunder and a bright flash of lightning stirred him awake. His eyes flew open…and he saw her. In that moment he saw the figure clearly – a woman, standing at the foot of the bed and looking at him.

His blood seemed to turn to ice, causing his heart to freeze in his chest. Then another flash of lightning, and another glimpse of the woman. He could tell right away that she wasn't human…at least, not *alive*.

The flashes of light continued far off in the distance, enough to allow Bill to see the apparition raise its arm to point at him. Then a ghastly voice came from the thing.

"Don't take my furniture," it said.

Bill watched with wide eyes, fear causing them to water. He watched as the apparition said its words and then just…vanished. It was as if the figure was suddenly made of smoke and a faint wind had come in to blow it away.

Bill bolted up from the bed and ran to the staircase, down it, and then out the front door of the lighthouse. He was pelted by rain from the storm as he raced toward the dockside shed.

Sleeping with the boats and tools and nets is better than sleeping with ghosts, he thought as he rushed through the stormy weather.

He made it to the shed, bolted it shut, and huddled in a corner with his coat tightly about him and his eyes locked on the door. He didn't get another wink of sleep that night.

~~~
~~~

Bill got up with the first rays of light, tired and groggy from his sleepless night. He waited on the dock for the world to lighten enough for him to feel comfortable going back to the lighthouse. He still had a job to do, and he meant to use every hour of daylight he could to get it done. He had no intention of staying another night at the place.

It was a bit past noon when the men finally got the last of the furniture tied down on the boat. You wouldn't know it from the sky, however. The clouds were dark and swirling above, like last night's storm was just a warmup to the blow still to come. The seas were turning rough, but no one thought it would be an issue if they were safe. And being safe meant as few men on the boat as possible. Being the senior most Coast Guard member there, Bill decided he'd do the duty himself.

The other men stood on the dock as Bill launched the small boat with the last few bits of furniture – some dressers, bedside tables, and the bed he slept in last night.

The going was easy at first, the waves tame as he got out past the breakers. But then the wind picked up, and the seas turned rough. The waves got larger and started pummeling the boat with their wrath. Bill's hold on the boat became tighter.

Yet still the seas increased. Another wave came, and then a second from the opposite direction. The boat rocked and shook and Bill lost balance completely. The boat went one way, he the other. Next thing he knew, his head was underwater and his nose and mouth were full of salt and brine.

"Ugh!" he gasped, getting his head up. He looked about and saw the boat capsized, the furniture bobbing in the surf...at least the pieces that were of wood. The rest was likely sinking to the bottom and–

Something tugged on Bill's foot, throwing him from his thoughts and back into the moment. It lurched on his ankle, and he reached down to feel a rope there.

Then it tugged again, and this time it pulled him under. His eyes went wide and the surprise of what was happening nearly caused him to gasp, losing all of his precious air. He had sense enough to realize that one of the heavier pieces of furniture that'd been tied down had somehow gotten its rope wrapped around him. Now that piece was plummeting to the bottom of the channel between the mainland and the island…at least a hundred feet down. It was taking Bill with it, and unless he did something quickly, he'd be dead.

Panic took hold. He looked up and saw glimmers of sunlight, now far above him, very far indeed. He managed to push the panic aside and reached for his belt knife. He got hold of it, pulled it loose, then fumbled to get the blade open. He fumbled too much. The knife fell from his fingers and vanished into the murky depths. He wanted to scream out loud. Instead he frantically pulled on the rope…but only for a moment.

A light appeared in the distance, materializing out of the darkness. Somehow the fear and the panic subsided enough for him to focus…and see the same ghostly figure he saw upon waking up in the lighthouse.

"I told you not to take my furniture," it *said* to him, though he heard no words and didn't see the ghost's lips moving. The words were just in his head.

It lasted just a moment, then the ghost vanished from sight and the fear and panicked rushed back in.

Bill tugged and tugged at the rope pulling him down until his lungs couldn't hold what little air he had left. With a gasp he let out the air and breathed in the salty seawater, and with it death. His eyes glazed over into nothingness.

THE END

ABOUT THE AUTHOR

Greg Strandberg was born and raised in Helena, Montana, and graduated from the University of Montana in 2008 with a BA in History. He lived and worked in China following the collapse of the American economy. After five years he moved back to Montana where he now lives with his wife, young son and daughter. He's written more than 80 books.

3 – The Sex Fiend

Janet Shumair noticed the man looking at her, and her pulse quickened. She didn't need the "female Viagra" anymore – it was permanently in her blood.

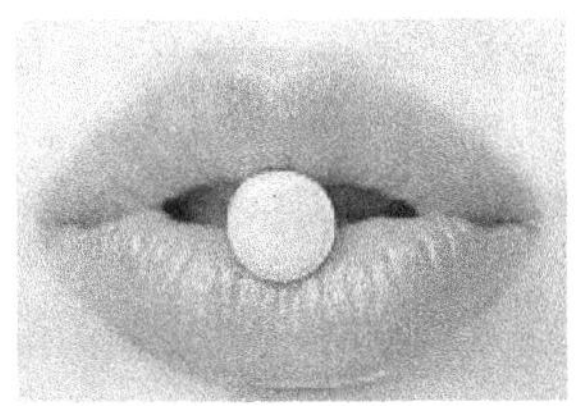

It hadn't always been this way for Janet. She'd been a successful news reporter, one of the big network TV variety. She'd traveled coast to coast and country to country, profiling the big stories, the headlining issues. Of course, none of that had left her much time with Mike at home, himself straddled with a full-time job, not to mention their two kids. It seemed each time she got home from the latest assignment, one or the other of them was 'out of the mood.' And it wasn't Mike, either, Janet knew — it was herself.

Janet looked both ways quickly and then darted across the street, toward the terminal doors. The man had given her a few more glances, and was now reaching for his phone. *Good,* Janet thought, *he's checking his phone, looking at his schedule, seeing if he has time for me.*

'You never have time for me!' that's what Mike had shouted at her when she'd rolled over in the bed, he storming off to whatever internet porn site he preferred. What could she say? She just wasn't in the mood.

That'd all changed in June of 2015 when Feboosterin was approved. It was toted as the "female Viagra," the wonder drug that would finally give women their sexual desire back. Janet had profiled a couple living on the Oregon Coast, a pair that'd been hampered by the same work-family juggle that she and Mike were experiencing. It'd worked for them, why wouldn't it work for her? Janet had popped her first pill that weekend.

BEEP! BEEP…BEEP!

Janet made it past the last lane of honking traffic and onto the sidewalk in front of the terminal doors. The man was walking down the sidewalk, but he was still glancing over his shoulder at her. He was talking on the phone now, too. *Good,* Janet thought, *he's calling his wife, telling her the flight was stuck on the runway, not to pick him up for another 30 minutes.*

'God, I hope this lasts at least 30 minutes,' Janet had said that Saturday night back home in the bathroom, just before she swallowed the Feboosterin pill. The kids were sleeping at friends and Janet had been adamant she and Mike spend the night together, dinner and a movie, and then upstairs. Of course it'd been more than 30 minutes, a lot more, and together with Mike's Viagra it'd been the best night of her life.

After that it was Feboosterin pills each night, and sometimes even on weekend afternoons. Janet and Mike's whole life changed, but for

Janet, it soon wasn't enough. Just taking Feboosterin on the weekend afternoons wasn't cutting it, soon she was taking it *every* afternoon, and going into the backrooms of the TV studio with several of the hired hands, set boys, and interns. Soon it was producers too, and then she was screwing just so the word wouldn't get out. It became too much, and she decided to stop taking Feboosterin. It was hard, but she made it through a full day, though the headaches were worse than here worse period had ever been.

Janet wasn't alone. She was soon doing stories on women who were taking Feboosterin, women that were turning into sex-crazed nymphomaniacs, though *her* network never called it that. Soon employers around the country were laying off women in droves, mainly because they'd been more focused on nailing the boss – or just about anyone – than actually getting any work done. It became an economic crisis. It became a medical crisis soon after.

The man was glancing over his shoulder more and more, and Janet was close enough now that she put on her million dollar smile and picked up her pace.

"Hey, handsome, how about we have some fun, huh?"

The man looked over his shoulder then tried to bury his head in his chest. *A shy one*, Janet thought, but then she caught a snippet of the man's conversation.

"…she's right behind me now, she's got the look in her eye, oh God…I don't want to be raped!"

Shit! Janet thought, then turned around and started moving back the way she'd come. It was still early in the day, there'd be plenty more…*shit – police*!

"Ma'am, please come over here right this instant!" the police officer said, reaching for his gun. He had 'Security' on his coat, so Janet knew he wasn't the real deal. She could make it, she could–

ZAP!

"Ugh!" Janet cried out as 50,000 volts of electricity shot into her.

"Got her!" the officer yelled to his partner, who was already calling in the medical unit.

Janet was down on the ground, the Taser still coursing through her. It was over, she was done. It took them less than half an hour to get the medical unit there, get Janet carted off to the nearest facility. The facilities were filling up fast, and many in the larger cities were overflowing. Unlike Viagra, Feboosterin had gone not to a woman's reproductive area, but to her brain. It'd turned them into lunatics, raging sex fiends.

Janet Shumair was one.

THE END

134

Read more of these stories…buy *Soul Catcher* on Amazon today!

There's a secret underground alien base in New Mexico, one sanctioned by the federal government. But that base got away from the military in 1975. Now it's 1979 and time to take it back. Discover *Dulce Base* today!

It's 400 BC and Seven States vie for power in the land that will become China. Marquis Wen of the State of Wei seeks to consolidate his power, and a successful siege helps with that. The other states, however, have him in their sights. Visit *The Warring States* today!

It's been a month since the 276 schoolgirls were kidnapped in Nigeria, and the president is taking flak for doing nothing. When an al-Qaeda bomber is spotted it's the excuse the CIA needs to go in and *Bring Back Our Girls*.

Flight 370 disappeared in March 2014. The dark shadow government that controls the world hijacked it. Now it's heading toward New York. Find out what happens in *Flight 370*.

It's the summer of 1973 in Hong Kong and a serial killer is on the loose. Each time he kills he leaves a card on the body. Now Inspector Jim Sharpe has to figure out why. If he doesn't, it could mean the end of the Hong Kong Police Force. Find out why in this thriller novel!

It's been six months since the horrendous incident atop Mount Misery, the incident that broke Beldar Thunder Hammer's band of adventurers apart. Now Beldar's putting the band back together. Why? To head back up Mount Misery to end the Kingdom's Hireling system for good. A tale of epic fantasy adventure unfolds, one you won't want to miss!